A Heart Full of Hope

ROBIN JONES GUNN

BETHANY HOUSE PUBLISHERS
MINNEAPOLIS, MINNESOTA 55438

A Heart Full of Hope
Revised edition 1999
Copyright © 1992, 1999
Robin Jones Gunn

Edited by Janet Kobobel Grant
Cover illustration and design by Lookout Design Group

"An Apple-Gathering" and "Twice" by Christina Rossetti are from *The Complete Poems of Christina Rossetti*, vol. 1 (Baton Rouge & London: Louisiana State University Press, 1979).

Focus on the Family books are available at special quantity discounts when purchased in bulk by corporations, organizations, churches, or groups. Special imprints, messages, and excerpts can be produced to meet your needs. For more information, contact: Resource Sales Group, Focus on the Family, 8605 Explorer Drive, Colorado Springs, CO 80920; or phone (800) 932-9123.

A Focus on the Family book published by
Bethany House Publishers
A Ministry of Bethany Fellowship International
11400 Hampshire Avenue South
Bloomington, Minnesota 55438
www.bethanyhouse.com

Printed in the United States of America by
Bethany Press International, Bloomington, Minnesota 55438

Library of Congress Cataloging-in-Publication Data
Gunn, Robin Jones, 1955–
    A heart full of hope / Robin Jones Gunn
       p.   cm. — (Christy Miller Series)
    Summary: Sixteen-year-old Christy is swept off her feet by Rick, a handsome Christian boy who wants to go steady with her; but her friendship with Todd makes her decision a difficult one.
    ISBN 1-56179-719-7
[1. Christian life—Fiction. 2. Interpersonal relations—Fiction.] I. Title. II. Series: Gunn, Robin Jones, 1955–   Christy Miller Series ; #6.
PZ7.G972He   1992
[Fic]—dc20

                                  92–18029
                                      CIP
                                      AC

02 03 04 05 06 07 08 / 15 14 13 12 11 10 9 8 7 6 5

To the youth group
at the First Evangelical Free Church of Reno:
May the Lord bless you and keep you.
The Lord make His face to shine upon you
and give you His peace.

Contents

CHAPTER ONE

Dazzling Dream Date

"Come on, Christy, try to not blink." Katie patiently held the mascara wand.

"I'm trying, Katie, but it's hard." Sixteen-year-old Christy Miller looked up at her red-haired friend and scrunched up her nose. "Why don't you let me do this part?"

"What would be the point of having me do your makeup for your big date if you end up doing everything yourself? Now hold still and look up." Katie carefully twirled the wand on the eyelashes lacing Christy's blue-green eyes.

"This feels weird, Katie."

"Hush. Look up. I mean it, Christy, don't move!" Katie finished the right eye and started on the left. "Good. Now don't blink. Let it dry."

Stepping back to examine her work, Katie smiled and said, "Perfect! Rick is definitely going to call you 'Killer Eyes' tonight."

Christy adjusted her five-foot-six-inch frame on the edge of her bed. For almost an hour she had patiently endured Katie's complete makeover, which included cucumber slices on her eyes while her nails were painted. The cucumbers were Christy's idea—something she had read in a magazine. As the article promised, her eyes had felt cool and refreshed.

That was before Katie started with the eye shadow, eyeliner, cover stick, and mascara. Now her eyes felt a little thick.

"You don't think you used too much eyeliner?" Christy asked.

"Not at all. Take a look." Katie handed her the mirror.

"Oh no!" Christy laughed as she looked at her long nutmeg-colored hair, now filled with hot rollers. "I forgot about these brain fryers. Do you think my hair is sufficiently cooked? I mean, look at me, Katie! I look like some kind of space alien wired for communication with my home planet."

"Yes, my little martian. Your hair is now a toasty golden brown and ready for a comb out. First, tell me what you think of your makeup."

"I don't know. I've never worn this much before. It doesn't feel normal."

"Good!" Katie snatched back the mirror and grabbed a blush brush. "This is not a normal date, so you're not supposed to look normal." She swished the soft brush over Christy's cheeks. "There! Now let's start on your hair before the space shuttle makes connection and lands in your backyard."

"Very funny. You sure you know what you're doing?"

"Yes. Now hold still."

Christy could feel herself getting more and more nervous the closer she was to being ready. After being "buddies" with Rick for so long, Christy wasn't sure how it would feel being dressed up and eating dinner at a fancy restaurant with him tonight. Or what the 90-minute drive from Escondido to Newport Beach would be like.

"You're not getting nervous now, are you?" Katie asked.

"Ouch!" Christy squeaked, pulling away from Katie's aggressive hair combing.

"Sorry, but I have to hurry. You only have half an hour until he gets here."

For five days Christy had avoided asking Katie her opinion of this date with Rick. Now, with the time melting away, so was Christy's courage. Knowing how opinionated Katie could be, Christy finally ventured the dangerous question: "Do you think I'm doing the right thing by going out with Rick?"

"You've been looking forward to this since he promised you this special date months ago—in a phone call from his vacation in Italy, I might add."

"I know, but do you think it will make things different between Todd and me?" Christy crossed and uncrossed her long legs beneath her bathrobe and listened to the swishing sound her nylons made.

"That depends," Katie said. "Todd knows you're going out with Rick, doesn't he?"

"No. Of course not."

Katie stopped combing. "Christy, I thought you said you talked to Todd yesterday, and he knew you were going to spend tonight at your aunt and uncle's in Newport Beach. Didn't you happen to mention to him that the reason you were going to be in Newport was because Rick was taking you to dinner there?"

"Well, no."

The two friends locked gazes. Katie's green eyes demanded an explanation.

"See, Todd called to ask me to a party at Tracy's house tonight, so I told Todd I couldn't go to the party. Then I told him I'd be at Bob and Marti's tomorrow, and he said he'd come by the house around noon. He didn't ask why I was going to be there, so I didn't tell him."

When Katie's expression didn't change, Christy continued. "What was I supposed to do? I couldn't cancel my date with Rick. He's going away to college next week. And why should I tell Todd about it?"

Katie went back to fixing Christy's hair.

"It's only a dinner, Katie! I don't have to ask Todd's permission. I'm sure it wouldn't matter to him at all. He's not the jealous type. You know that!"

"Hey, relax! You're going to mess up the perfect job I did on your makeup." Katie started in on Christy's hair. "I'm here, aren't I? Supporting you, helping you get ready. I'm on your side, Christy. I'm not saying anything against Todd or Rick. It's your choice. Close your eyes. I'm going to spray your hair."

Christy obliged, tilting her chin down so Katie could spritz her bangs. Mentally, she convinced herself there was nothing wrong with being interested in two guys at the same time. How could she possibly cause problems with Todd by going out with Rick? Neither of the guys would know a thing about the other. She'd have a nice dinner with Rick tonight and then spend tomorrow afternoon with Todd. Simple.

The problem was Katie. Katie had never been a big fan of Rick's. Even though she was being sweet and supportive, if she really spoke her mind, she would slash Rick into ribbons, saying he was a smooth talker, a show-off, and not the kind of guy Christy should be going out with—especially since Christy already had a guy like Todd in her life.

"Your dress!" Katie exclaimed. "We should have put it on before I did your hair. I know, try to step into it."

Katie pulled Christy's black dress off the hanger and

unzipped it. It was a dress Christy had only worn twice because it made her look and feel too grown-up. She wasn't sure she was ready to dress like that. But it had been Katie's first choice for what Christy should wear tonight. Even Christy's mom had agreed it was the right dress for a formal dinner.

Katie held out the dress as Christy carefully stepped into it.

"Perfect," Katie declared, zipping up the back. "Don't move a muscle, Cinderella. I'm searching for your glass slipper."

Christy laughed. "I think you're into all this more than I am."

"I like all this froo-froo stuff. Just because I'm not the one being invited on dream dates to romantic restaurants doesn't mean I can't enjoy the part of the fairy godmother."

Katie hunted for Christy's black shoes in her closet while Christy examined her hair in the mirror.

"You're sure it's not too froofy?"

"What?" Katie asked. "Your hair or your dress?"

"Either. Both. I don't know. All of me. Are you sure I look all right?"

Katie joined Christy in looking at her reflection in the mirror above her antique dresser. "You look dazzling!" Katie summarized.

"Dazzling?"

"Yeah, dazzling! This is how you should look. You're not going for fast food with Todd. This is a real date."

Christy took a deep breath and smiled. "Okay, you're right. I'm relaxed. I'm going to have a great time. Everything is going to be wonderful."

"Not just wonderful," Katie said. "Dazzling!"

Ten minutes later, when tall, dark-haired Rick arrived and handed Christy a long-stemmed red rose, she began to believe

Katie could be right. This could be a dazzling evening.

Christy felt a little embarrassed when her mom and dad made them pose for pictures, but she knew she would be glad she had them later. Mostly she wondered what Rick thought of her. Did she look all right? Did he like the dress? Her hair?

Rick, the all-around athlete, stretched his six-foot-two-inch frame with a serious expression as Christy's dad gave him strict instructions that Christy must be to Bob and Marti's house by 11:00. Rick agreed, shook hands, and held the front door open for Christy.

Right before swishing out the door, Christy turned around and blew a tiny kiss off her index finger. The kiss flew down the hall to Katie, who was hiding in Christy's room with the door open a crack.

"You look beautiful," Rick said, opening the passenger door to his '68 Mustang.

Christy slid onto the upholstered seat. For one quick second she flashed on how different this was from all the times she had hopped into Todd's battered Volkswagen van, "Gus the Bus."

You're with Rick. Get Todd out of your head.

"You look really nice, too," Christy said as Rick got into the car. He had on black slacks, a crisp white shirt, and a black jacket.

"I especially like your tie," Christy added, reaching over and feeling the unique tie. In keeping with Rick's flashy side, it looked as if someone had thrown a handful of fluorescent confetti at him and it had all stuck on his tie.

"You like that?" Rick said. "I got it in Italy. Thought it might add a festive touch to our evening, Killer Eyes." Then giving Christy a smile that said, "I've been looking forward to this date for a long time," Rick turned the key and roared down the quiet street.

Lifting her rose to draw in its rich fragrance, Christy thought, *No, this isn't a normal night. Katie, you were right. Tonight is going to be dazzling!*

When Rick Got on His Knees

"Here we are!" Rick announced an hour and a half later as he turned the car into the restaurant's driveway. The place looked like a charming old Italian villa. "I told you I'd find the best Italian restaurant in Southern California, and this is it—the Villa Nova." Rick pulled up behind a Cadillac and waited for the valet to come park his car.

As Christy wondered if she should bring her rose with her, her car door opened, and the valet extended a hand to help her out. Without looking up, she grabbed her purse and the rose with one hand, and let the young man pull her to her feet by her other hand.

Instead of letting go of her, the valet suddenly wrapped his arms around her and, with a wild hug, roared, "Christy, I can't believe it! How are you doing?"

She vaguely recognized the voice, but since her face was now buried in the guy's shoulder, Christy was at a definite disadvantage. He pulled away. She looked up and saw his face and then viewed Rick's puzzled expression.

"Doug!" Christy caught her breath and smoothed down her hair. Todd's best friend was the last person she had expected to see this evening. "I'm so surprised! I haven't seen you in a long time."

"You look awesome, Christy! What's the occasion?" Doug asked, an exuberant smile lighting up his tanned face.

"Doug, I'd like you to meet Rick. Rick, this is Doug." Christy hoped the introductions would help her avoid having to give any explanations.

The guys shook hands good-naturedly, and Doug jumped right in. "This is so awesome that you're here tonight! We're having a party at Tracy's. You guys have to come. You remember how to get there, Christy?"

"Well, actually...," Christy fumbled for the right words, feeling a panic rising in her heart and pounding through her veins. This was the same party Todd had asked her to. She couldn't show up there with Rick.

Before she could get out any words, Rick answered for her. "Sure. We'll come. I've been wanting to meet some of these beach friends Christy talks about."

"Cool!" Doug said. "I'll see you there when I get off at 9:30."

Rick tossed Doug the keys to park his car. Doug jogged around to the driver's side and said, "Awesome Mustang!" Then, before folding himself into the driver's seat, he leaned over the roof and said, "This is great, Christy! Everyone is going to be so surprised to see you."

"Yeah," Christy mumbled as Rick slipped his arm around her and led her into the restaurant. Everyone would be surprised, all right—especially Todd.

"So, who's that guy? Another one of your old boyfriends?" Rick asked.

"Doug? No, no, not at all! He's just a friend of ..." Christy caught herself. "... Tracy's. He's friends with Tracy. That's the girl who's having the party. They used to go out, but now they're just friends."

"And now he's looking for a new girlfriend," Rick said.

"I don't know. I don't think so." Christy could feel her heart still pounding as the hostess led them through the labyrinth of tables. Rick's questions weren't helping her calm down a bit.

"My guess is, he's looking for a new girlfriend, and you look pretty good to him."

The hostess stopped in front of a window table that looked out on Newport Bay. Rick pulled out a chair for Christy, and she seated herself. He pushed in her chair, leaned over, and whispered, "But you can tell Doug to give up, because you're already taken."

Christy gratefully accepted the menu held out to her. She opened it and hid her flaming red face behind its tall barricade.

I can't believe this is happening! What am I going to do? Why is Rick saying these things?

"What sounds good to you, Christy? You can't go wrong with any of the pasta dishes here, I've been told." Rick then rattled off a list of Italian names from the menu, complete with authentic accent. "Now this sounds good," he said, reading the name of another Italian dish. "What do you think?"

Christy shyly peered over the top of the menu and managed a weak smile and a nod. "Sure." Her voice came out cracked, so she cleared her throat and tried again. "That sounds good."

"Then that's what we'll have," Rick stated, snapping closed his menu.

What did I just order? It could have been squid brains for all I know! Everything is coming at me so fast. I want to go back to how things were in the car on the way here. I want to feel dazzling again.

Christy closed her menu and groped for the rose on her lap,

automatically drawing it to her nose to sniff. Maybe its fragrance would bring back the magic.

Rick reached over, wrapped his hand around her wrist, and pulled the flower over to his side of the table. Taking a whiff, he smiled and said, "It's sweet, but not as sweet as you."

Christy felt charmed but not charmed enough to calm the frantic confusion raging inside. She wanted to move the conversation to a neutral subject. The view out the window, maybe. She turned her head and was about to make a comment on how pretty the summer evening light looked, dancing on the water; but Rick had other ideas.

Still holding her wrist, he took his other hand and gently began to pick the lock on Christy's "Forever" ID bracelet. It was the bracelet Todd had given her last New Year's.

"What are you doing?" Christy asked, keeping her voice light.

Without looking up, Rick said smoothly, "You don't mind, do you?"

He'd already released the clasp and now held the gold bracelet in his fist. "Guys are funny. We like to know that when a girl goes out with us, she's not bringing along mementos from past relationships."

"It's not like that, Rick," Christy began. How could she explain her relationship with Todd to Rick when she'd never been able to explain it to herself?

"Then what *is* it like?" Rick looked up, melting her with his gaze.

"Todd and I are good friends. We have been for a long time."

"But you're not going together, right?"

"Well, no."

"Todd goes out with other girls, right?"

"Well, yes, he has."

Rick took Christy's hand in his and held it firmly. "Then let me have a fair shot, okay? You don't mind not wearing that chain tonight while you're with me, do you?"

Rick laid the bracelet on the table and released Christy's hand. She knew the next move was hers. She knew what Rick wanted her to do.

Christy gingerly picked up the bracelet and slipped it into her purse. Looking up, she tried to echo the smile Rick beamed at her. Inside she felt overpowered, as if Rick had just burst into her heart and broken the lock on the treasure chest where she kept all her secret feelings. She didn't want him breaking in like that. But more important, she didn't want him to go away.

At that moment the waiter appeared, and the tension dispersed. Their water glasses were filled, and a basket of garlic bread was placed before them.

Christy eagerly began to nibble on the bread while she listened to Rick talk about his summer trip to Europe. As long as she kept chewing, she wouldn't have to answer. Rick seemed satisfied to keep talking as she smiled and nodded at the appropriate times. It gave her a chance to calm down and think.

By her third piece of bread, Christy had come to a conclusion. *I'm being far too immature and emotional about all this. This is Rick. I am having dinner with Rick. I want to be here. Why am I worrying about Todd? Nothing has changed between us just because I'm not wearing his bracelet. I'm going to have a good time tonight, and there's nothing wrong with that. There's no reason I should be upset.*

"Good bread, isn't it?" Rick asked.

Christy nodded and realized she had emptied the basket.

"I'll have them bring some more," Rick offered.

"Oh, no, really, that's okay," Christy said quickly. "I should save room for the dinner. It is good, though."

Feeling calmed and ready to pay more attention to Rick, Christy hoped he wouldn't ask her any questions about what he had been talking about while she did her soul-searching. She had no idea what he had said. Maybe it would help if they moved to a new subject.

"Tell me about school," Christy said. "When do you leave, what classes are you taking, and all that."

Rick jumped right in with a full rundown of all his freshman courses at San Diego State.

"You realize, don't you, that even though I leave on Tuesday, I'm only going to be an hour away. That means I'll be back in Escondido every weekend."

"That's good," Christy said absentmindedly.

"I don't think you catch my drift here, Christy. I'll be home every weekend, and I plan to spend every weekend with you."

Christy didn't respond.

Her face must have given away her surprise, though, because Rick laughed and said, "Yes, Christy, I'm asking you to go out with me. You know, 'go together,' 'go steady.' Or like my brother says about his girlfriend, I want you to be my 'significant other.' "

Christy still didn't have a response for him.

"Why are you looking at me like that? Am I doing this the wrong way? Wait. I know." Rick scooted his chair back.

Then, stepping over to Christy's side of the table, he dropped to one knee, took her hands in his, and said in a gentle voice, "Christy, I've waited a long time to ask you this. I've never felt for another girl the way I feel for you. Will you go out with me?"

Christy felt as if her heart had stopped beating and the whole world had come to a standstill, waiting for her to answer him. All she could feel was Rick's firm grasp enveloping her shaking hands. All she could see were his soft brown eyes pleading with her to say yes.

"Yes," she suddenly squeaked, and the world began to move again.

The couple at the table next to them smiled and applauded softly. Rick confidently returned to his seat. Leaning across the table, he said, "I was hoping that's what you'd say."

What just happened? I thought this would be a simple dinner. A one-date thing, and now I just said I'd go out with him! How did that happen?

Just then their salads arrived, and once again Christy could keep her mouth full so she didn't have to talk. Rick enthusiastically told her his ideas for their future dates.

Christy smiled and nodded and halfway listened. She only halfway did everything for the next hour. She had gone numb.

After dinner, Rick ordered a dessert for them to share and coffee for both of them. Christy loaded her coffee with cream and sugar and then took about three sips. She poked at the elegant chocolate dessert with her fork, eating only one bite.

The numbness didn't leave Christy until they stood outside the restaurant waiting for the valet to bring the car. Sure enough, it was Doug who brought Rick's red Mustang around to the front.

"Perfect timing," Doug said, hopping out and handing the keys to Rick. "I get off in two minutes. You guys want to wait a second, and you can follow me over to Tracy's?"

Christy shriveled inside. *Oh, Doug, why did you have to bring that up? I was hoping Rick would have forgotten all about it.*

"Sounds good," Rick said, opening the door for Christy.

In a few minutes Doug's yellow truck swung around in front of them, and Doug motioned with his arm out the window for them to follow.

"You know," Christy said, drawing up all the strength and courage she could find, "we really don't have to go to this party. You won't know any of the people there, and it's not as though they're expecting me or anything. Besides, I have to be at my aunt and uncle's in about an hour and a half, so we wouldn't have much time there, and—"

"Hey, it's okay," Rick interrupted, reaching over to give her a little pat on the leg. "I know what you're trying to say, Christy. Some guys get freaked out when they meet all their girlfriend's friends. It won't be like that with me. You'll see. I've waited a long time to be your boyfriend. I'll make you proud of me. I promise."

Christy's grip on the rose tightened when he called her his girlfriend. When he said he had waited a long time to be her boyfriend, her tensed finger found a small thorn toward the top of the rose.

Then, with a bump, Rick pulled into Tracy's driveway. Without warning, the thorn sliced into Christy's flesh.

CHAPTER THREE

The Luckiest Girl in the World

"Ouch!" Christy held up her finger. Just enough light shone on the cut for her to see a few drops of blood.

Rick turned off the car's engine. "You okay?" He pulled a tissue from a box under his seat, wrapped it around her finger, and examined the rose. "That's pretty cheap," he complained. "You'd think they'd know enough to cut off the thorns before they sell these things. Are you okay now?"

Without making any noise, Christy had been crying uncontrollably from the instant the thorn had pricked her. She couldn't stop the tears from streaming down her cheeks.

"Oh, you're crying," Rick said, as tenderly as if she were a small child. "Come here." He offered her another tissue with one hand and wrapped his other arm around her.

"I'm okay, really," Christy sniffed, pulling away so that Doug wouldn't see them wrapped up together. "I'll go rinse it off in the bathroom."

Opening her own door and springing out, she hurried up the steps to Tracy's house. Christy glanced back and saw Doug standing by Rick's car, the two of them talking.

To her relief, Tracy's front door stood wide open. Christy

slipped in without anyone seeing her. She knew right where the bathroom was and disappeared inside, locking the door behind her. As if she had reached her own private refuge, she let more tears flow.

What am I going to do? What are we doing here? I've messed things up so badly, they'll never be straightened out. What does Rick think of me? What will Todd think?

A knock at the door made her jump. She ignored it, hoping the person would go away.

"Christy? Are you okay? It's Heather."

Christy hadn't seen Heather since last Christmas vacation. But she wasn't sure she wanted to see her or anyone until she had her feelings figured out.

"Christy? Will you let me in?" Heather knocked persistently.

Christy gave in and unlocked the door. Wispy, blonde Heather burst in, pouncing on her with a warm hug. Christy quickly locked the door behind Heather.

"Doug said you were here!" Heather said in her breathless, excited way. "And who is that guy with him? Have you seen him? He's gorgeous! You're crying! What's wrong? And what's on your finger? What happened?"

Wiping away the tears, Christy explained, "It's really nothing. It was a thorn. I should have realized it was going to happen." Christy looked away and stared at the shower curtain, talking aloud as if Heather weren't even there. "With the rose comes the thorn. I should have known. I thought I could have one without the other, but it doesn't work that way. Why did I think I could just go to dinner, and it wouldn't be a big deal?"

"What in the world are you talking about, Christy? Are you totally freaking out on me here?" Heather tugged on Christy's sleeve. "Turn around, Christy. Look in the mirror."

Christy looked and discovered that Katie's superb makeup job had dissolved into two rainbow rivers winding down her cheeks. At this moment she looked anything but the part of Rick's "Killer Eyes" girlfriend.

Heather giggled and handed her a washcloth. "You'd better wash that stuff off before it dries on permanently. Now explain to me how you got here. Todd said you couldn't come."

Plunging the washcloth under the running water, Christy said, "It's a bizarre story."

"Good, I like bizarre stories. Did you come with Doug?"

"No, I actually came with Rick, the other guy. We went out to dinner at Villa Nova and just happened to see Doug."

"You mean you're on a date right now with that gorgeous guy? What's his name? Rick? Oh, Christy, you have to be the luckiest girl alive!"

"Yeah," Christy said sarcastically. "I'm so lucky that I'm now going with him."

"What?" Heather squealed, grabbing Christy by the elbow and squeezing it so hard that Christy dropped the washcloth. "When did this happen? Does Todd know?"

"No, of course not. Rick asked me tonight at dinner." Christy explained the whole situation as she washed her face and blotted it dry.

Heather listened to every word, wide-eyed and open-mouthed. "I was right. You're the luckiest girl in the world."

"I don't feel that way," Christy said with a sigh. "I feel as though I'm in a huge mess."

"Why? Rick is a Christian, isn't he?"

"Yes, of course."

"Then what's the problem? Todd? Do you really think Todd would ever treat you the way Rick has—roses and dinner and saying he would wait until your parents would let you start dating? Think about it, Christy!"

"I don't know. I like Rick, but I've liked Todd for a long time."

Heather put her hands on her hips and said, "You are 16 years old. A young woman. In some cultures, you could be married by now. You met Todd when you were 14, and you had a huge crush on him, am I right? A lot has changed since then. You've changed; Todd has changed. Face it, Christy, Todd is never going to be the kind of guy who takes a girl out to dinner. Don't let his blond, blue-eyed surfer looks fool you. He's not a normal guy. He wants to be a missionary, you know."

"I know."

"Todd is the kind of guy who'll probably never marry. He'll spend his life among the natives, sleeping in a hammock, eating bug larvae, and saving the souls of people in the jungle who have never seen a white man before. He'll probably win a Nobel Peace Prize and die in some headhunter's stew pot."

"Heather!" Christy interrupted her dramatic friend with a laugh. "What is the point here?"

Heather looked Christy straight in the eye and said, "Don't you see? The point is, you *want* to go out with Rick. You want to be his girlfriend. Deep down, you've wanted it all along. Otherwise, when he asked you, your heart would've said no, and you would've turned him down. You said yes to Rick because you *want* to be his girlfriend. Can you deny that?"

Christy took a deep breath. She thought about the way Rick had treated her so tenderly when she pricked her finger in the car. Todd never would have responded that way. Todd never had said the things to her that Rick said tonight. Rick wanted her to be his girlfriend, and yes, maybe deep down she liked the thought of him being her boyfriend.

"I don't know, Heather. You could be right."

"It's just hard because you probably feel bad about Todd finding out this way. That's not your fault. You didn't try to make it happen like this. Besides, I've known Todd a long time, and I hope I don't hurt your feelings when I say this, but Todd will probably get over you a lot quicker than you'll get over him. He's that way."

"You could be right."

They both were silent for a moment, and then Heather said, "Come on. Everyone's anxious to see you. Let's go join the party and let whatever is going to happen, happen."

Christy rummaged in her purse for her cosmetic bag and did a quick fix on her makeup. Then, with Heather nudging her out the door, she walked slowly down the hallway.

When they entered the living room, Christy saw Rick but not Todd. Rick had wasted no time in becoming the center of attention to a circle of six girls.

"Look, you guys!" Heather broke Rick's spell on them. "Christy's here!"

"Hi!"

"How you doing, Christy?"

"You look great!"

Each girl had a warm greeting, but none of them moved from her spot. Turning back to Rick, they urged him to continue his story.

Rick looked up briefly, shrugged his shoulders, and gave Christy a wink.

"Come on," Heather said. "Tracy's in the kitchen. Let's go in there."

Yeah, and Todd's probably in there, too. Am I ready to face him? What am I so nervous about? Everything Heather said made sense when she said it. Why don't I feel convinced now?

Tracy had her back to them, pulling out soft drink cans from the refrigerator. Turning around, she closed the door with her foot.

That's when Christy caught a glimpse of Todd, sitting in a kitchen chair, talking to Doug.

"Christy!" Tracy threw her arm around Christy's neck in a hug, almost knocking her in the head with a soda can. "Oh, I'm sorry!" she laughed. "I'm so glad you're here. Todd said you'd be at your aunt and uncle's tomorrow, but I didn't think you could come tonight."

Doug jumped into the conversation from his chair next to Todd. "Yeah, I told them how I found you and Rick going through the trash cans at my restaurant and how I felt sorry for you and brought you here."

"Very funny," said Heather. "Just because you guys don't know the meaning of taking a girl out for a nice dinner doesn't give you the right to make fun of those who do."

Christy suddenly remembered the last time she had been with these friends for a party. It was last New Year's, and she had worn this same black dress. Only that night she had come with Todd. And that was the night Todd had given her the bracelet. Right now, it all seemed like a lifetime ago.

She couldn't look at Todd. To make sure their eyes didn't meet, she kept looking down at her wound, pretending that her finger needed much more attention than it did.

Tracy followed her line of sight and said, "Do you want a Band-Aid for that? We have one right here." She pulled one out of a drawer.

I think I might need a Band-Aid for my heart. If I look at Todd, my heart will start bleeding all over the floor.

As soon as the Band-Aid was in place, Tracy handed Christy a soft drink and said, "Come in my room. I want to show you something."

Christy gladly turned her back on Todd and followed Heather and Tracy. Tracy shut the door, flipped on the light, and turned to Christy with huge eyes. "Where did you find *him?*"

"Rick?"

"That's Rick? The one you told me about from your school? I couldn't believe it when Doug said you guys were having dinner at the Villa Nova! And look at you. You're so dressed up! Tell me everything."

Christy began the story again for Tracy while Heather willingly filled in any missing details. Tracy listened carefully, and Heather concluded with the part about how Christy must have really wanted to be Rick's girlfriend or else she wouldn't have said yes when he asked her.

"Is that how you feel?" Tracy asked.

"I think so. Everything has happened so fast, I'm not sure what I feel."

"He seems like a really nice guy and a perfect gentleman," Tracy said. "I didn't realize you liked him this much, though."

"It's weird. We were friends for so long because I wasn't old enough to date, so it never became anything more."

"Isn't that the best way for relationships to be?" Heather said. "Friends first, then boyfriend and girlfriend?"

"I guess. I've never been in this situation before."

"I think you're in the best situation possible. You're good friends, he's older than you, he's totally gorgeous, and he's a Christian, too! What else could you ask for?"

When Heather said that, something melted inside of Christy. Heather was right. What more could she ask for? Why was she holding back? She should feel honored that Rick had picked her and waited so long to date her. It would be foolish to let her crush on Todd keep her from experiencing a real relationship with a guy who *wanted* to be her boyfriend and had already proved, more than once, how much he cared for her.

With her heart beginning to fill with excitement, Christy explained, "He's going to San Diego State, so we'll see each other only on weekends. He's got all these fun ideas of things for us to do. He said he started to make lists of ideas for dates more than six months ago, since he had to wait so long for me to be old enough to date."

"I ask you," Heather said with her eyes all sparkling, "what other guy on this planet would do that? He sounds like a dream come true. I'm glad you woke up quickly enough to realize it! And see how much better you feel about everything now that you've thought it through? You should have heard her in the bathroom, Tracy. Rambling on about how roses have thorns. I thought she was going to pass out on me!"

Christy laughed. "I wasn't used to the idea of having a boyfriend, I guess. You know what I was thinking, don't you? Rick is like the rose, but having to see Todd and everything was like the thorn."

Tracy's heart-shaped face took on a serious expression. "You were right, Christy. That's exactly how going steady is. It's a rose with a thorn, because when you break up, either you get hurt or the other person gets hurt. There's no way around it." Then she added thoughtfully, "Most of the time, you both get hurt."

Heather cheerfully interrupted, "That's why I said you shouldn't think it's a problem with Todd. I mean, how can you break up when you two were never really going together? It's not the same thing as what you've got with Rick."

Just then someone tapped softly on the door. "I hate to break it up in there." Rick's voice came through the closed door and filled Tracy's bedroom. "But I need to get my girlfriend home."

" 'Girlfriend,' " Heather whispered, and the three of them made gleeful faces and squeezed each others' arms.

"I'll be right there, Rick," Christy answered.

"You'll be at your aunt and uncle's tomorrow, right?" Tracy asked.

Christy nodded, pushing away the thought that she was supposed to meet Todd at noon tomorrow.

"Do you want to try to get together?"

"Sure. I'll be around, and I don't have anything else going on." *Now that I've shown up here with Rick, I'm sure Todd won't be calling me tomorrow.*

"I'll give you a call, then," Tracy promised and opened her bedroom door.

Rick stood in the hallway with his arms folded across his chest, comically looking up at the ceiling and whistling. "Oh, Christy," he said, "the invisible party girl."

"I'm sorry. We were just talking."

Rick took her by the hand and led the way to the front door. "Bye, everyone. Nice meeting you. We'll see you later!" he called out as they made their exit.

Doug surfaced from the kitchen, but Todd stayed behind. Something in the back of Christy's mind said, *See? If Todd really cared about me, he'd try to talk to me before I left. If he really wanted a relationship with me the way Rick does, he'd fight for me. But he's letting me go. He doesn't really care, and he'll never care for me the way Rick does.*

Doug shook hands with Rick and said, "Hey, we'll see you on

campus next week. Christy, you didn't tell me your boyfriend was going to my school."

"You let me know if that other guy drops out of your apartment," Rick said. "I'd much rather live there than in the dorms."

"I will," Doug promised. "He has until Monday to turn in his money, and if he doesn't, he's out of there. It'd be great to have another Christian in our apartment.

This is too bizarre. It's like Rick is stepping in instantly to take Todd's place in my life, even by buddying up with Doug.

Rick waved to all the girls, then whisked Christy out the door and to the car. "Now, tell me how to get to your aunt and uncle's."

Christy directed, and Rick drove the few blocks to the beach-front house.

"We only have a few more minutes before you have to go in," Rick said. "How about a quick walk on the beach?"

"You're sure we have time?"

"Positive. Come on!" Rick opened her door and, taking her hand, led her down the pavement to where the sand began.

They slipped off their shoes, and Rick put them on top of a concrete-block wall. "Remind me where I'm leaving these," he said, grabbing Christy's hand again and pulling her onto the sand.

"Come on!" he shouted and began to run, tugging Christy along beside him.

"Wait! Wait!" Christy cried out, coming to a halt next to a fire pit. "I'm getting sand in my nylons!"

Rick laughed as she tried to brush off the sand. Christy cautiously sat on the rim of a fire pit and wiggled her toes to get rid of the particles. She looked up at Rick, then, noticing her surroundings, jumped up from the edge of the fire pit as if it had suddenly turned hot.

I can't believe it! Of all the fire pits on the beach, why did I stop by this one? I shouldn't be here with Rick. This is where Todd and I had breakfast on Christmas morning!

"Come on," Christy said, sprinting toward the water. "I'll race you!"

They ran through the sand together until they were a few yards from the water's edge. Rick, with a spurt of energy, sprinted ahead of her. Turning at the shoreline, he opened his arms and caught Christy.

"No fair," Christy said breathlessly. "The sand in my nylons slowed me down."

"So, what do you want? Best two out of three?"

The lacy edge of a wave crawled up and without warning grabbed their feet with its cold fingers.

Christy let out a tiny squeal of surprise and scampered up to higher ground.

"Look," Rick said, following her and pointing up to the sky, "it's a wishing moon."

Christy looked at the tiny sliver of bright alabaster. "A wishing moon?"

"Yeah," Rick said, "there's so little of it left you have to quickly make a wish on it before it completely disappears."

Christy smiled. "When my brother was little, he used to call that kind of moon 'God's fingernail' because it kind of looks like a fingernail when you bite it off. I remember the first time he saw it like that, and he said, 'Hey, God bit off His fingernail and left it in the sky.'"

Apparently not too amused by her story, Rick said, "Come on. Close your eyes and make a wish."

Christy played along, tilting her head toward the moon and

closing her eyes. Before she could think of what to wish for, Rick kissed her.

She opened her eyes and saw Rick grinning.

"I got my wish!" he said.

"We'd better get back," Christy said quickly. Everything was going too fast again, and she wanted to retreat to the safety of her room at Bob and Marti's so she could think it all through.

"I'm sure we have more time," Rick said, reaching over and holding Christy. "Come here and tell me what you wished."

Christy nervously pulled away. "I don't want to be late. You know how strict my dad is. I really don't want to get in trouble."

"Okay, okay," Rick said, letting go. They turned to walk back, and he slipped his arm around her shoulders. "You cold?"

"Not really." The truth was, she was burning up. After running and being kissed like that and now meshing her feet through the sand with Rick's arm around her, how could she possibly be cold?

Christy wrapped her arm around Rick's middle. She had always felt tall and awkward because of her height. At this moment, with her arm around Rick and his strong arm around her, she felt petite and secure.

"How are you getting back to Escondido tomorrow?" Rick asked.

"My uncle is going to take me."

"You tell him to save his gas money. I'll come get you."

"But, Rick, it's an hour-and-a-half drive."

"So?"

"You don't have to come back for me." Christy could feel his arm tighten around her shoulders, and she knew it was pointless to object.

"What time do you want me to come?"

"I don't know. What's convenient for you?"

"I'll be here at 5:00," Rick said as they arrived at the pavement and he retrieved their shoes.

Christy noticed someone standing on the sidewalk by Rick's car, looking down the street. They walked a few feet closer, and she realized it was her uncle.

"Good evening," Bob said in his dry way as they met him at the car. "Nice night, isn't it?"

"It's not 11:00 yet, is it?" Christy asked, hiding her embarrassment that her uncle was outside looking for her.

Bob checked his watch. "Eleven twenty-seven, to be exact. Will you be needing help with your luggage, ma'am?" He played the part of the hotel doorman perfectly, but Christy could tell she was in trouble.

Rick unlocked his car and handed Christy's overnight bag to Bob. With a friendly smile, Rick said, "Good evening, sir. I'm Rick Doyle."

"Oh, I'm sorry," Christy said quickly. "Rick, this is my Uncle Bob. Uncle Bob, this is Rick. But then, you probably figured that out already."

As she stumbled over her words, the two men shook hands, and Rick explained that he would be back to pick up Christy tomorrow.

"Well, I'll see you tomorrow night," Christy said, feeling unsure of how to say good-bye to Rick with her uncle standing there. She waved, and Rick waved back.

"Five o'clock," Rick echoed and then got into his car.

Christy followed her uncle to the front door, and even though she didn't try to think of Todd, she couldn't help being flooded with memories of when he had walked her to this front door. He had kissed her while they stood on this porch.

The minute Christy and her uncle stepped inside the house, petite, dark-haired Aunt Marti appeared, wagging her finger at Christy. "You'd better count your lucky stars that you have an uncle who covered for you tonight, Christina! Where were you? Your father called at 11:05 to make sure you were here, and we had no idea where you were!"

Christy felt sick to her stomach. "What did you tell him?"

Bob's calm voice overrode Marti's anxious scolding. "I'd seen you pull up a few minutes earlier, so I knew you were here. I figured you two were taking a little moonlight stroll. I was young once. I know these things."

"All I can say is, it's a good thing your father didn't ask to speak to you, or you would've been in real trouble!" Marti warned.

"I'm sorry," Christy said. "I wasn't wearing a watch, and Rick said we had enough time."

Bob and Marti exchanged a look that Christy didn't know how to interpret. Marti remained silent, and Bob picked up her bag and began to carry it up the stairs.

Over his shoulder, Bob said, "Guess you might as well decide now."

"Decide what?" Christy said, following him up the stairs.

"Decide if you're going to believe everything that young man tells you."

CHAPTER FOUR

Later, Christy

It didn't take Christy long to fall asleep that night. She wanted to put Rick's rose under her pillow but discovered she had left it in his car along with her purse. That didn't bother her, because she knew she'd see him tomorrow and they'd pick up where they had left off.

Even though she went to bed after midnight, she woke up at 5:15 and couldn't go back to sleep. After rolling around for half an hour, she gave up and got out of bed. Drawing back the sheer ivory curtains, Christy looked out at the beach, feeling like a bird surveying the land from its lofty perch.

The deserted beach had always intrigued her with its vastness. She especially liked it in the early morning light when a thin puff of fog floated in from the ocean, giving the sand a soft, hazy halo. Everything outside her window looked like a dream world, and this morning it beckoned her to come walk in its stillness.

Following her impulse, Christy slipped into her jeans and sweatshirt and tiptoed downstairs, out into the morning mist. The brisk dampness made her shiver, and she wished she had a jacket. To warm up, she began to jog, feeling the sand fill her tennis shoes.

She trotted along the firmer sand by the shoreline and thought of how fun it had been racing to the water's edge with Rick last night. Maybe they could go for another walk tonight. She wanted to feel his arm around her again and hear him say how much he liked her.

Yes, she told herself, *Rick definitely makes me feel things I've never felt before with any other guy. This must be what Heather was talking about—it's the difference between a crush and a real relationship.*

Her lungs filled with damp air as she ran. Then a fit of coughing made her stop and sit for a moment in the sand. She had come quite a way down the beach and decided to catch her breath before jogging back. Hopefully, she would be able to sneak into the house unnoticed and go back to sleep for a few more hours.

Her mind and emotions didn't feel any more settled than when she awoke. At least the jogging had helped to tire her body some.

Christy was about to leave when she noticed another jogger coming toward her through the lifting fog. For the first time, she felt afraid of being alone on the beach. She realized it had been a foolish thing to take off on her own like that. She also realized that she would be more noticeable if she suddenly jumped up and started to run ahead of this person. With her heart beating rapidly, she decided to stay put and hoped the person wouldn't notice her.

Wrapping her arms around her drawn-up knees and keeping her gaze down, she thought, *Keep going, keep going, whoever you are. You can't see me. I'm invisible.*

The thumping of the jogger's feet approached. To her terror, the foot-pounding stopped right in front of her. She knew the person was now standing still, examining her.

"Oh, Lord God, protect me!" she whispered under her breath.

The person slowly stepped closer and sat down beside her. She could hear heavy breathing.

Without looking up, and before a word was spoken, Christy knew the person sitting next to her was Todd. All her feelings crumbled like a sand castle does when the rising tide rushes in on it.

What is he doing here? Why is he out at 6:00 in the morning? Did he have trouble sleeping, too? Is this a nightmare or a God-thing? I can't look at him. What am I going to say?

They sat silently for a long time as Christy listened to Todd's breathing slow to an easier pace. He didn't move. She didn't move. Her back began to hurt from being hunched and looking down for so long.

Worst of all was the way she shivered uncontrollably from the damp cold while everything inside her shouted *Todd, can't you see that I'm cold? Why don't you put your arm around me?* But she knew he never would. She knew Todd well enough to know that he was probably praying right now and not thinking of how to make her feel more comfortable or secure.

Christy practiced a dozen opening lines in her mind. None of them made it to her lips. What could she possibly say? "I want to break up?" How, when they weren't really going together? She couldn't symbolically hand him the "Forever" bracelet and take off running down the beach, because she'd left it in her purse in Rick's car.

She could feel the thumping of another jogger coming toward them and used the opportunity to lift her head and look at the passerby.

"Good morning," the older man called out to them. "Beautiful morning, isn't it?"

"Good morning," Todd yelled back, breaking the silence.

To her surprise, the instant she heard Todd's rich voice, something rumbled deep inside her, and she began to cry. She blinked and swallowed hard, but the tears kept coming. Struggling to find her voice, Christy whispered, "I'm sorry."

Suddenly, everything seemed to clear in her mind, and she prepared herself to say the truth that was on her heart. She knew she had ignored it until this moment. Now was the time to speak it as openly as she felt it. She wanted to go back to the way things were with Todd. Last night had been a one-night date with Rick. She was not going to go steady with him. She was not his girlfriend. She would never go out with him again, ever. She only wanted to go out with Todd. She wanted to be Todd's girlfriend. She'd always wanted to be Todd's girlfriend.

"I . . . ," Christy began, "I know last night it looked as if I were trying to be Rick's girlfriend or something, but that's not how it is. It was just a date. I'm not going with him. It doesn't change anything about the way I feel about you."

"I know," Todd said.

Christy caught a small breath and kept going, afraid that if she stopped she'd never say what was on her heart. "I don't know exactly how to say this, Todd. I've tried before, and I've never been able to find the right words." Christy took a long, deep breath. "I really, really like you. I care for you in a way I've never cared for anyone else in my life. I . . ." She knew she wasn't ready to use the word *love,* yet there had to be something stronger to say than "like." She couldn't produce such a word. "I really, really like you, Todd. I hope you can understand what I'm saying." Christy felt as if she'd just ripped her heart out of her chest and was holding it in her hand, waiting for Todd to take it.

"I do understand what you're saying, Christy." Todd paused, then spoke quick, deliberate words, as if he'd practiced them all night. "But you've got two more years of high school ahead of you, and you should feel free to date whomever you want and not think you have to apologize to me for it. It was selfish of me to think that I could hold on to you and wait for you to grow up."

His words hit her like a bucket of icy saltwater in the face. All her vulnerable, transparent feelings of a few seconds ago flip-flopped to instant fury.

Wait for me to grow up? What does he think I am? A baby?

The tears changed, too, into hot, angry pellets. Without thinking, she blurted out, "Well, that's fine. I'll mail your brace-let back to you, then."

"No. It's yours to keep. Remember what I said when I gave it to you? No matter what happens, we're going to be friends for-ever. I meant it then, and I mean it now."

This is unbelievable! Christy thought, wiping her tears. *I pour out my heart, and he tells me to grow up! And I can't even have the satis-faction of breaking up, because he won't take the bracelet back.*

They sat in silence, with apparently nothing else to say. Then in true Todd-like, bizarre fashion, he placed his cool hand on Christy's forehead and said, "May I bless you?"

"Bless me?"

"Christy," he began, without waiting for her approval, "may the Lord bless you and keep you. May the Lord make His face to shine upon you and give you His peace. And may you always love Jesus first, above all else."

Bless me? Christy thought as Todd pulled his hand away. *Make His face shine on me and give me peace? I'm anything but peaceful right now! Todd, you spiritual geek, why don't you take me in your arms and tell me you love me and that you'll fight to get me back?*

Todd stood up.

What? That's it? I hand you my heart, you tell me to grow up, and then you give some kind of benediction to make it all right. Now you're going to go, just like that?

Todd wedged his feet in the sand and surveyed the waves with his arms folded across his broad chest. "I'm going to Oahu," he announced.

Christy sprang to her feet. "What?" It was one thing for him to give his "blessing" to her to date other guys, but news of his moving away filled her with a desperate sense of losing him forever.

"I've decided to hit the surfing circuit with Kimo, like he and I always talked about when we were kids. I called him last night, and there's room for me at his house on the North Shore. I'm leaving tomorrow."

"Tomorrow? Todd!" Christy's fearful, angry feelings ignited her words. "Why? What is going on here with you?"

He briefly explained, "I'm going to U of H; registration is Monday."

"You mean the University of Hawaii? Why are you going there?"

"So I can get in a semester of school before the local surfing competition cranks up. That should keep my dad happy."

Keep your dad happy? What about me? I'm not happy you're leaving. And what about you? Do you really want to do this, or did you just decide last night when you saw me with Rick?

"Todd, what's going on? With you, with us? What's happening here?"

He turned to meet her tearful gaze. Those silver-blue eyes that had embraced Christy's a hundred times now held her at a distance as they clouded with a watery mist.

"We're changing, Christy. That's all. We're both changing."

Before she saw it coming, Todd's arms surrounded her in a

fierce hug. Then he turned and forced his way across the sand.

"Todd!" she called out, but he kept moving away from her.

Run after him, Christy! Throw your arms around him. Talk him out of going to Oahu. This is your last chance! Do something!

Her mind barked its commands, and her emotions raced at a terrifying speed, yet her feet refused to move. Her throat closed up, and she stood frozen and speechless as Todd, with each step, moved away from her.

"Bye, Todd," she whispered into the thin morning air.

When he was several yards down the beach, Todd turned around, and wiping his eyes quickly with his forearm, he gave his usual chin-up gesture.

"Later, Christy," he called out, and the sound of his hoarse voice hung heavy in the air like a call from across a great chasm.

CHAPTER FIVE

Holding Hands

Sleep, Christy told herself as she trudged through the sand back to Bob and Marti's house. *I need some sleep; then I'll be able to think this whole thing through, and I'll know what to do.*

Her plan to slip back in bed backfired when she encountered her aunt and uncle seated at the breakfast table.

"Are you trying to give me gray hair, Christy?" Marti snapped. "First, you push your curfew last night, and then you're not even in our house six hours before you sneak out again! Where were you, and who were you with?"

Christy had never seen her aunt this furious. "I . . . I couldn't sleep so I went for a walk."

"Alone? Do you know how dangerous that is? What were you thinking, young lady?"

Bob stood up and put his hands on Christy's quivering shoulders. Looking into her tearful eyes, he calmly asked, "Are you okay?"

Christy couldn't decide if she should clench her teeth and turn into a rock or break down and sob all over her uncle. She ended up slipping by with a question. "Could you please excuse me? I need to use the bathroom."

She exited quickly and heard her aunt say, "That's it? You're going to let her go just like that?"

Christy locked the door to the bathroom adjacent to her bedroom. Curling up into a shivering ball in the corner, she cried until she had no tears left. Everything inside and outside ached. She forced herself to take a steamy shower and let the hot water massage away the pains.

When the tips of her fingers began to wrinkle, she shut off the water and wrapped her pink flesh in a thick terry cloth robe. Her bed had never felt so inviting before. Now, if only her aunt would leave her alone long enough so she could get some sleep. She rolled over on her side and curled up, falling into an exhausted sleep.

A persistent tapping on the bedroom door awoke her some time later.

"Yes?" she answered, trying to focus her eyes.

"Tracy's on the phone for you," Uncle Bob said through the closed door. "Do you want to talk to her?"

Christy propped herself up on her elbow and answered, "Sure, I'll be there in a minute."

"I have the phone right here," Bob said. "You want me to bring it in?"

"Sure, thanks."

Bob stepped into her room and, before handing her the cordless phone, said softly, "You ready for me to bring up some breakfast?"

Christy smiled and nodded at her tenderhearted uncle. "Thanks."

He winked and disappeared, closing the door behind him.

"Tracy?"

"Hi. What did I just hear? You're getting treated to breakfast in bed? You never told me you had a personal slave."

"My uncle's like that, Tracy. You know him; he likes to baby me, and I let him. Believe me, this morning I need all the babying I can get."

"It's almost afternoon, I hope you know. And how rough could your morning be if you're still in bed?"

Christy explained her early morning encounter on the beach, carefully choosing her words, since Todd and Tracy were such close friends. For some reason it didn't sound as much like the end of the world as it had felt a few hours earlier.

"Todd called me an hour ago," Tracy said. "He didn't even tell me he saw you this morning."

See? Just like Heather said. I'm taking this much harder than Todd. He's already acting as though nothing happened.

"But you know," Tracy continued, "he didn't seem completely himself. I mean, he acted all excited about going to Oahu, but I wasn't convinced he really felt that way. He'll probably get more into his adventure once it starts happening. He's definitely leaving tomorrow, though. Did he tell you that?"

"Yes."

"I don't know why, but somehow I feel it's the best thing for him right now. And I don't think it's because of you and Rick. He's talked about going on the surfing tour ever since I've known him. I think it's the kind of thing a person has to do when the opportunity comes along. He needs to get it out of his system."

"I guess I should be glad for him that he has this chance," Christy said.

Tracy paused and said, "He told me he's glad you're going out with Rick."

Christy thought she had already cried all the tears her body had. Not so. A fresh reserve of them bubbled up. In a wild gush, she poured out her heart to her friend.

Bob knocked on the door just then and said, "I'll leave this tray out here. You can get it whenever you're ready."

Christy cupped her hand over the phone and weakly called out, "Thank you." Then she wiped her eyes and blew her nose. "Listen to me," she said to Tracy. "I'm a mess!"

"You have a lot going on, and no time to think it all through. You're doing fine, considering the circumstances."

"But I've completely ruined my relationship with Todd!"

"No, you haven't. Todd doesn't give up on any of his friends, ever. He'll never turn his back on you. Remember, it's not as though you broke up. Your friendship went into a different phase, that's all. You're changing, as he said. You're giving each other room to grow."

"How? How am I helping him grow? He's the one who told me to grow up."

"Don't you see, though? If you hadn't come with Rick last night, Todd might never have been prompted to make that final decision to go on the surfing tour. The opportunity may. have passed him by, and in a few years, he would have regretted it."

"Tracy, I think you're saying all this to make me feel better."

"Oh, really? Well, how am I doing?"

"Not bad, I guess. You have me smiling at least. Hang on a second. I'm going to grab my breakfast from the hallway."

Christy brought the tray of fruit, orange juice, and a blueberry muffin back to her bed and snuggled under the sheets. She and Tracy talked for almost an hour, and by the time they hung up, Christy felt more settled about letting Todd go.

After all, he was part of her past, and now it was time to move on to a real relationship with a guy who thought she was wonderful. Obviously, Todd didn't see her that way or he would have tried to win her back from Rick. Todd cared more about surfing than he did about her.

Slipping into a pair of cut-off jeans and a sleeveless T-shirt, Christy ventured out on the back patio. Marti, wearing a stylish black and ivory sleeveless dress, sat in the shade of the table umbrella, going through a cookbook and affixing yellow sticky tabs to certain pages.

Pulling the lounge chair around so she faced Marti, she plunged right in. "I'm sorry about last night and this morning, Aunt Marti. You were right. It wasn't a very wise idea for me to take off by myself. I promise I won't do it again. I'm really sorry."

Marti let out a sigh. "I suppose it's all part of growing up, dear."

"Yeah," she said, half to her aunt, half to herself. "Growing up seems to be my problem today."

Not catching any deeper meaning in Christy's statement, Marti continued. "Your uncle and I have tried to be lenient whenever you've stayed with us. And until now, you've been quite dependable. I would hate to see you lose your privileges due to irresponsibility."

"I know; you're right."

"You know we trust Todd completely. He's become like a son to Bob. But we don't know Rick, and although Bob said he seemed like a nice young man, you can't be too careful these days."

"Am I through getting yelled at?"

Marti looked offended. "I'm not yelling at you."

"I know, but you know what I mean. Because if you are, I'd like to ask you something," Christy said, shielding her eyes from the sun with her hand so she could see her aunt's reaction.

"You can come to me at any time with any question. You know

that. You've always known that. And you know I was not yelling at you."

"I know."

"So, what is your question?"

"Do you think I'm old enough to go steady?"

"With Todd? Certainly." Marti answered without a speck of hesitation and returned to her cookbook.

"It'd be a little difficult to go steady with someone who's moving to Hawaii tomorrow."

"What?" Marti's reaction assured Christy that she now had her aunt's full attention.

It took more than 20 minutes to give Marti the details. When Christy finished, Marti said, "Why didn't you tell me all this?"

"I did. Just now."

"This is a horrendous amount of decision-making for you to attempt on your own. You should have told me about Rick last night when you came in. And why didn't you tell us you were with Todd this morning on the beach? Christy, you must talk to someone about these things, and when your mother isn't around, you know you can always come to me."

"I know. I am. So what do you think? Am I old enough to go out with Rick?"

"Your mother will say no."

"I know. That's why I'm asking you." Christy could feel her legs getting sunburned and shifted to her side.

"I don't suppose you thought to put on some sunscreen?" Marti asked. "And are those the best shorts you have? You certainly can't wear those tonight when Rick comes to pick you up."

"I have a pair of jeans and a sweatshirt with me, too," Christy said, knowing her aunt was not going to give her a straight answer to her question.

She also knew Marti was about to make an announcement of some sort. It seemed to be her way of taking control. She always lifted one of her eyebrows before making a declaration.

"And what about school clothes? What are you going to wear next week when school starts? I don't suppose you've gone shopping yet, have you?"

"No. The first few weeks are always hot, and everyone wears shorts."

Christy knew what was coming. She'd been shopping plenty of times with Marti. Even though she didn't always welcome her aunt's indulgences when it came to clothes, today Christy was delighted with the idea of buying something new to wear for Rick when he came to pick her up. She'd never felt that way with Todd, but then Todd had never noticed or commented on her outfits the way Rick did.

Christy's prediction was correct. A wild and generous shopping trip was in her immediate future. They had only two hours, which turned out to be all the time they needed, since money was no object.

They arrived home with enough new clothes to last Christy the entire first semester. She felt excited at the thought of wearing a new outfit on every one of her upcoming dates with Rick.

At 5:00, Christy heard the doorbell ring and quickly pulled on her new jeans. They were more in style than any of her other jeans. Pulling them up and zipping them, she felt like a model.

At Marti's suggestion, Christy had brushed her hair to one side and fastened it back with some new combs. She had never tried her hair this way before, and it made her feel even more like a model.

Galloping down the stairs, Christy anticipated seeing Rick standing in the entryway. He told her once that he liked her in red so she specifically wore a new red shirt.

Instead of Rick, Alissa stood by the front door, chatting with Uncle Bob.

"Alissa!" Christy greeted her friend. "I didn't realize you were still here on vacation. And look at your hair! It's darling!"

When Christy and Alissa met on the beach last summer, Alissa's long, blonde hair had been a point of envy for Christy and half a dozen other girls. Alissa's gorgeous mane was now cut short. She turned around so Christy could see how cropped it was in the back.

"You like it? It's the new me. Everything else about me has changed this summer; why not my hair?"

"You look great! I'm so glad to see you. Come on in." Christy led the way to the plush living room sofa. Before they could sit down, the doorbell rang again.

"I'll get it," Bob called out.

Christy knew it would be Rick this time. She felt eager to see him and even more eager to introduce him to Alissa.

Alissa had had a rough year. She had become pregnant and moved away, had a baby girl, and then gave her up for adoption about a month ago. Right after that she had returned to visit California with her mother. That's when she gave her heart to the Lord. Alissa *had* changed a lot. Christy wanted her to meet as many Christians as possible, including Rick.

"Hello, ladies," Rick said, stepping into the living room and eyeing Alissa.

When Christy made the introductions, Rick said, "You'll have to come down to Escondido sometime."

"It would have to be tomorrow," Alissa said. "We're going back to Boston next week."

"Why not come with us tonight?" Rick volunteered. "Your

parents wouldn't mind if she stayed overnight, would they, Christy?"

"No, not at all. That really would be fun, Alissa. I was hoping to spend some more time with you before you left."

"Thanks, but I've already got something going on tonight. Doug called, and they're having some kind of surprise going-away party. That's why I stopped by. Doug told me you were here, and I thought we could go together."

"Going-away party?" Rick asked.

"It's for Todd. He's leaving tomorrow for Hawaii to go to school or surfing or something. Anyway, Doug is trying to throw a party together, and I told him if it was for Todd, I'd be there. Have you met Todd, Rick? He is the most incredible guy."

"Yeah, I've met Todd, all right. So he's leaving, huh?" Rick's grin looked a little too smug for Christy. At the same time, she felt relieved that Rick had heard about Todd this way. It would prove to Rick that she was completely available to be with him. If Rick believed Todd was a part of the past, maybe Christy could believe it, too.

"Do you both want to go with me?" Alissa asked.

Rick looked as if he were about to answer for them, the way he'd answered Doug last night, when Marti made a grand entrance.

"Actually," she said, "we have other plans. I'm sure you two girls will be able to get together in Escondido, don't you think, Christy?"

"Sure. I'll draw you a map to my house, Alissa. Come anytime tomorrow after church, like around 1:00. Okay?" Christy excused herself to find a piece of paper.

Bob met her at the kitchen doorway with a pad of paper in his hand and a concerned look on his face. "You sure you want to let Todd go just like that? Marti told me about this morning on the beach. Are you sure you don't want to try to smooth things out? I could entertain Rick if you and Alissa want to go to Doug's."

"No, it would only make things worse. It's better this way. Really. Todd and I will always be friends. I'm dating Rick now, and I wouldn't want to be rude to him and put him off after he drove all the way up here." With each word, Christy further believed she was right.

"You're sure?"

"Yes, I'm sure. You'll like Rick, once you get to know him. Really."

"Apparently your aunt is going to see to that. She's made plans for the four of us to have dinner in Laguna Beach." Bob handed her the pad of paper, and Christy quickly drew the map.

"Thanks," she said.

"Don't thank me," Bob mumbled. "I'm not sure I'm doing you any favors."

After all the plans were settled and Alissa said good-bye, Marti turned to Rick. In her sweetest voice, she said, "I hope you don't mind my making dinner plans for us?"

"Not at all. It was actually very kind of you, Mrs.—"

"Oh, please, call me Marti."

Right then and there, Christy knew her aunt was smitten by Rick's charm. Now if only Bob would give his approval.

That was Christy's hidden goal during dinner. More than once she tried to get Rick onto a topic that sparked an interest in Bob. It proved to be quite a challenge, since Bob seemed to be taking her "breakup" with Todd personally.

The food at the quaint restaurant Marti picked out on the Pacific Coast Highway was delicious. The atmosphere, with the beach only a few yards away, was delightful, and being with Rick was dreamy.

Marti did everything she could to keep the conversation light and cheery. Christy played along, even though she thought her aunt was acting as if she and Christy were friends out on a summer night double date.

When Rick finished eating, he leaned back in his chair and rested his arm across the back of Christy's chair. As the four of them talked, Rick's warm hand rubbed the back of her neck. Christy loved feeling adored. This was what she'd always dreamed it would be like with a boyfriend.

"How about a stroll?" Marti suggested. "Most of the shops along here are still open. What do you think?"

"Sure. Sounds good to me," Rick said, standing and offering Christy his hand.

She felt so secure slipping her hand in his and feeling his strong fingers wrap around hers like a blanket. Rick held her hand firmly during their entire walk, and Christy loved it.

The only time he let go was in a pottery shop when he found a vase.

"Here," he said, carrying it to the cash register and fishing for his wallet, "you're going to need this."

She laughed at his impulsive manner and wondered what he meant. The vase was rather masculine-looking, with black streaks across a dark blue ceramic base. It looked handmade and earthy. She didn't particularly like it.

Rick's mysterious statement made sense when they returned to Bob and Marti's and loaded all her things into the back of Rick's car. On the front seat a bouquet of red roses awaited her.

"What are these for?" she asked shyly after Rick had started the car.

"For my girlfriend."

"They're beautiful," Christy said, nuzzling her nose into their velvet petals.

"Not nearly as beautiful as you. You look like my red rose tonight. Did I tell you how good you look? I like your hair like that. Not that you should wear it that way all the time, but tonight it looks good. Makes you look older."

"Does it make me look too much older? I mean, does it make me look like I'm trying to look older?" Christy asked, suddenly feeling self-conscious.

"Not at all," Rick said. "You look just right. I like it when a girl takes the time to make herself look good for her boyfriend. It shows she really cares about him, and she cares about what people will think of him when they see her with him. And the way you look, I'd never be embarrassed for people to see us together."

I know he meant that as a compliment, but somehow it didn't sound exactly right. Was he trying to warn me that I should always make sure I look good when we go out? It's a good thing Marti just made a major contribution to my wardrobe!

Rick reached over and took her hand. She felt close to him, warm and secure. She wanted that feeling to last all evening. She wanted him to hold her hand all the way home.

Driving with one hand, Rick put a CD in the player, and for an hour, mellow saxophone music rolled all around them. They didn't speak the whole time. They just held hands and let the music lull them. Christy closed her eyes and rested her head against the seat.

So this is what it feels like to have a boyfriend who adores me. I love it. I never knew it could feel this wonderful. Don't ever end, sweet night. Don't stop driving, Rick. Don't stop the music. Don't ever stop being my boyfriend.

Rick's car came to a stop, rousing Christy from her half-dream state.

"Where are we?" she asked, looking around at the darkness outside the car window.

"Look out there," Rick said, pointing over the hood of the car. "The beautiful lights of downtown Escondido."

"I thought we were going to my house," Christy said, stretching the kink in her neck and trying to hide the nervous feelings creeping into her voice. "We really should get going."

"Is your neck sore? Here, turn around. I'll get the knot out."

Christy turned, and Rick's strong hands massaged her neck, then her shoulders. She felt herself beginning to relax beneath his touch. He leaned over and kissed her lightly on the neck, then again on the cheek. When he turned her face to kiss her on the lips, she pulled away and put up her hands in defense.

"Wait." It was all she could think to say. "Just wait."

Rick sat silently waiting, while she collected her thoughts. Then he asked, "What is it, Christy? What's wrong?" His voice sounded gentle and patient.

"This is coming at me too fast, that's all. I'm just not ready for this."

Rick let out a low chuckle. "Ready for what? I was only going to kiss you. Honest."

Christy remained on guard, with her back pressed against the passenger door, frantically trying to evaluate her colliding emotions.

"Hey," Rick said, "don't look so frightened. It's only me, remember? Rick, your boyfriend. I'm not going to hurt you. Come here." He opened his arms and drew her to him in a gentle hug.

His hand stroked the back of her hair, and in her ear, he whispered, "You smell so good. You feel so good in my arms. Do you know how long I've waited to hold you like this?''

He tilted up her chin, and this time she let him kiss her. As soon as he did, the panic feeling in the pit of her stomach returned.

She pulled away, more slowly this time.

"I'm sorry, Rick. I'm not feeling well. My stomach kind of hurts, and well, I'm just not ready for all this.''

Rick pulled back and let out a huge puff of air. Folding his arms across his chest, he said, "It's that surfer guy, isn't it?''

"No.'' Christy shook her head and looked Rick in the eye. "Todd and I were never like this. I told you. He and I were very close friends. That's all. You're my first real boyfriend, and well, maybe I don't know how to act like the perfect girlfriend. But if you take it slow and give me a chance, I'm sure I'll get used to all these feelings rumbling around inside my stomach right now.''

"So,'' Rick said with a slow grin returning to his face, "I make you sick to your stomach, do I?''

Christy let her smile return. "You know what I mean.''

He reached over, grasped her hand, and squeezed it. All her fearful, overpowering feelings gave way to the more comfortable, warm, close feelings.

"Come on, Killer. I'll take you home,'' he said.

CHAPTER SIX

Restrictions

Several minutes later, when Rick and Christy pulled up in front of her house, Christy wondered what time it was and if her parents were still up. Rick carried her luggage and extra shopping bags to the front door, while all Christy carried was her purse, her bouquet, and her new vase.

The minute they stepped on the porch, the front door swung open, and Christy's dad stood behind the screen door looking like a grizzly bear. He didn't say a word, only opened the screen door and grabbed Christy's suitcase out of Rick's hand.

"Well, good night, Christy," Rick said quickly. "Good night, Mr. Miller." Then he vanished, leaving Christy to face her parents alone.

She stepped inside, her bouquet cradled in one arm, the ceramic vase in the other. "I'll put these in water," she said, feeling her mother's glare following her into the kitchen.

"11:47" blazed out from the digital clock on the microwave.

It can't be that late! No wonder my parents are in a nuclear melt-down! I'm supposed to be home by 10:00 except for special occasions. If I explain carefully, maybe they'll consider this a special occasion. Then again, maybe I'm in big trouble.

Haphazardly cramming the roses into the vase, Christy decided to leave them on the kitchen counter. Plopping them in the middle of the kitchen table would *not* add a festive touch.

With cautious steps, she returned to the living room and sat down on the couch at the opposite end from her mother. This was not Bob and Marti's, where she could excuse herself and retreat to her room. She knew she was about to receive the lecture of her life.

Mom went into the kitchen; Christy could hear her making coffee. Apparently, this was going to be a long night.

Alone in the living room with her dad, Christy broke the ice by asking, "Did Uncle Bob call to tell you Rick was bringing me home?"

"No. I called him several times." Dad's voice had a low growl to it that caused Christy's heart to beat faster. "I finally reached him at 10:00. He said you'd been out to dinner and that you left his house around 9:30. It is now almost midnight. Where have you been?"

"We stopped for a while and talked. Then Rick brought me home. We didn't stop for long."

"Just talked?" Dad's face was beginning to turn a shade of red that clashed with his red hair.

Mom stepped in just then and delivered a steaming cup of coffee to Dad. With a concerned look, Mom said, "Christina, we had absolutely no idea where you were. I had dinner prepared here for Bob and Marti, and when you didn't show up, and no one called us, and no one answered the phone there . . ." Mom choked up. "We thought the worst. Do you have any idea what you put your father and me through tonight?"

Christy lowered her head. "No. I'm sorry. I thought Bob called you."

"You should have called us," Dad said. "Just because you're old enough to date doesn't mean you can take off any time you want with anybody you want! You still have to ask us before you go out or make arrangements to do things. Is that understood?"

"Yes."

Dad drew in a deep, steamy sip of coffee before coming down hard. "You want freedom. You want to drive the car whenever you want. You want to date whomever you want, and you want to wear whatever you want. If you want freedom, then you have to show your mother and me that you are responsible."

Christy glanced at her round-faced mother, who gave her a stern look and quietly went back to drinking her coffee.

"First, you drove the car to your baby-sitting job three days last week, and when your mother went to the grocery store today, she nearly ran out of gas. When you drive the car, you are responsible to fill it with gas."

"But that job ended last week," Christy reasoned. "I've already spent the little I made, and when school starts next week, I won't have any money for gas."

"Yes, you will. You're going to find a job. Your mother and I talked about it, and if you want to drive the car, you need to find a job that will provide you with at least enough for gas money each week.

"Second," he continued without leaving any space for Christy to protest, "you will have to have approval from your mother or me before you go on any more dates. You'll have to tell us where you are going; you must be home by 10:00, even on weekends; and we must approve of the boy you're going out with. Understand?"

"Yes," Christy answered, relieved that he hadn't taken away her privilege to date. She and Rick could be home by 10:00 if they started out early enough. It really wouldn't change a thing.

"Next, where did you get that outfit? Those are not the kind of jeans I want my daughter wearing."

"But they're brand-new. Marti just bought them for me today. They're in style, Dad."

"Fine," Dad said. "If everyone is wearing them, you'll have no trouble giving away yours. *You* are not wearing them. Is that clear?"

Christy nodded and looked down at her jeans, thinking of how a few hours earlier she had felt like a model in this trendy outfit. Now she felt ridiculous. It was one thing for Rick to notice her outfits and another for her dad to.

"Final point is you're grounded for two weeks for your irresponsibility tonight."

"Norm?" Mom said softly. "I thought we decided on one week."

He tilted his coffee mug up for one last swig. "Any girl who comes home dressed like that needs two weeks' restriction."

Mom looked down at her coffee mug, which Christy knew meant her mom wouldn't press the issue anymore.

"We love you, Christy," Dad concluded. "You know that. But we can't say we're real happy with the choices you seem to be making lately. We care about you too much to let you toss away your virtue so easily."

His last line, "toss away your virtue," haunted Christy through her long and fitful night of sleep.

What does he mean by "virtue"? Does he think I'm doing something wrong with Rick? Or that my clothes aren't modest enough? I'm totally conservative compared with my friends. He'd die if he saw some of their outfits! Just what is virtue, and how am I tossing it away?

The next day when Christy's family arrived home from

church, Rick called to apologize for not meeting her at the service. He said his family had taken him out to brunch as a farewell before college. Christy quickly explained she was on restriction and needed to get off the phone.

"That stinks! What am I supposed to do for the next two weekends?" Rick grumbled. "I'm coming over. I'm going to talk your dad out of it."

"No, Rick, don't. You don't know my dad. You'll only make it worse."

"Christy?" Mom called from the kitchen. "I need your help with lunch."

"I have to go, Rick. I'm sorry. I'll talk to you later."

"When? If I can't call you or see you, how am I going to talk to you?"

"I don't know. I'm sorry. I need to hang up. We'll figure out something. It'll work out. You'll see."

"Yeah, I'll work it out. Don't you worry about anything, Christy. I'll work it out."

About 10 minutes later, as they were sitting down to a lunch of tuna melts and coleslaw, Rick showed up at the front door. Since it was so hot, the front door was open, and they could all see Rick standing by the screen door.

"We're eating, Rick," Christy's dad said without getting up from the table. "Christy is on restriction, so she won't be able to see you for two weeks."

Christy felt like a five-year-old whose best friend came over to play and was shooed away.

"That's what I'd like to talk to you about, sir. You see, I'm leaving for college on Tuesday, and I wondered if you'd reconsider and allow me to take Christy out tonight."

"No."

"Well, not 'out' exactly. I thought we'd spend the evening with my parents at my house. Would that be okay?"

"No."

Rick didn't know Christy's dad the way she did, or else he would have given up after the first no. The poor guy stood outside the screen door and tried at least five different approaches before saying with a sad puppy face, "Bye, Christy. Have a good first week of school."

She felt crushed and furious with her dad. Sometimes he didn't seem to give a rip about anybody else's feelings. What had her mother ever seen in him, anyway?

Christy picked at her lunch, eating only the cheese and a tiny pinch of coleslaw. She was about to excuse herself when another car pulled up in front of the house, and a girl with short blonde hair bounded up to the door.

Oh no! It's Alissa. I completely forgot she was coming today.

"Mom," Christy pleaded, "it's Alissa. I invited her to come before I knew I was on restriction, and she drove all the way from Newport Beach. She's leaving for Boston this week, and this is the only chance I'll have to see her probably ever again!"

"Hello," Alissa called out, tapping on the wooden frame of the screen door. "Is anyone home?"

"All right," Christy's dad said. "Let her in. But you're staying here. You're not going out anywhere."

Even though he sounded gruff, Christy could tell he really didn't mind Alissa coming to see her.

"Come in, come in," Dad said, getting up to open the screen door. "You must be the one who moved to Boston."

"Yes, I'm Alissa. It's nice to meet you, Mr. Miller." She looked pretty as usual, and she was losing some of the pudginess around her middle that had come with the pregnancy.

Christy stood up and introduced Alissa to Mom and Christy's little brother, David. Up to this point, David had been quiet, taking in all the afternoon's events.

Now he piped up. "How come Christy gets to have her girlfriends come over even though she's on restriction? That's not fair!"

Alissa looked sheepishly at Christy. "Did I come at a bad time?"

"No," Mom spoke up, "it's fine, really. You girls can go on back to Christy's room."

Christy automatically began to clear the table.

"That's okay. I'll get these," Mom said.

"That's not fair either!" David whined. "When it's my turn, I always have to do the dishes."

The girls retreated into Christy's room and closed the door. Christy flopped face first onto her bed. With her arms spread out, she hollered into the patchwork bedspread, "Aughhhhhhh!"

"Bad day?" Alissa ventured, gracefully alighting on the edge of the bed.

Christy talked nonstop for 20 minutes while Alissa patiently listened to her complicated dilemma with Todd and Rick and her parents and the restriction and having to find a job.

When Christy finally paused to catch her breath, Alissa smiled and said, "You don't know how blessed you are."

"Blessed?" It reminded her of Todd's "blessing," and right now that didn't help.

"Yes, you are blessed," Alissa said. "When my father died about a year and a half ago, I had no boundaries. I could do whatever I wanted. And I did. Who was going to stop me? My alcoholic mother? No one ever said, 'No, I won't let you do that. I care about you too much to let you hurt your future like that.' I wish I had then what you have now."

Christy instantly sobered. "I never thought of it that way."

"What are you going to do about Rick?"

"What do you mean?" Christy was more concerned about how she could get off restriction and how she was going to find a job. Rick seemed like the least of her worries. In two weeks, they could pick up where they had left off, and Christy had already imagined that they'd only appreciate each other more for the separation.

"Are you going to break up with Rick?" Alissa asked.

"Why would I want to break up with him?"

Alissa countered with another question. "Why are you going out with him?"

"Well, because we've been friends for a long time, and now that I can date, this is the next step in our relationship. Besides, this is what I've always wanted—a boyfriend. And Rick is a great guy. He really cares about me. I'd be crazy to break it off and give up all that for nothing."

"Christy," Alissa said gently, "I know exactly what you're saying about how good it feels to have a boyfriend and to be adored and desired and everything. But listen to me. It's not going to fill your heart."

"I'm not trying to fill my heart. I'm having a normal teenage dating relationship with a really great guy. That's all."

"Okay." Alissa readjusted her posture. "Then can I ask you to promise me something?"

"What?" Christy thought Alissa looked almost comical, she was so intense as she reached over and grasped Christy's right hand.

"Promise me you won't do any more than kissing—and I

mean light kissing—with Rick or any other guy you go out with. Promise me that."

"Alissa, that's not even an issue," Christy said. "I don't plan to ever get really physical with any guy until I'm married."

"And last Friday afternoon you didn't plan on going steady with Rick, did you?"

"Well, no," Christy said.

"But you let Rick talk you into something you weren't ready for, and it sounds as though you felt pressured to say yes."

"Maybe a little pressure, but Alissa, going steady isn't the same as getting physically involved."

"It's the first step. And if you said yes to going steady when it was completely Rick's idea, you could give in to Rick's ideas on how far you guys go physically. You have to draw a line, Christy.

"I have good reason to feel so strongly about all this, and you know it," Alissa said. "My biggest concern for you is that you're looking for a guy to fill your heart—first Todd and now Rick. A guy will never be able to meet all your needs. You have to want God with all your heart, soul, strength, and mind. As long as there's somebody else there to fill your heart or mind, you won't really fall in love with Jesus the way you would if He was all you wanted."

Now Christy felt angry. *Why are you, of all people, lecturing me like this? Wasn't I the one who led you to the Lord only a month ago? How come you're so instantly spiritually mature?*

Instead of voicing her feelings, Christy forced a smile and said, "I can see you've sure been doing some soul-searching this past month."

"Actually, I've been reading. I finished the New Testament, and I'm starting on the Old Testament."

"You read the whole New Testament?"

"Sure, haven't you?"

"Yeah, well, I mean, parts of it. And parts of the Old Testament, too."

When Alissa left two hours later, Christy hugged her and said, "Thanks for all the advice."

She meant it. Even though Alissa's directness was hard to take, Christy knew she spoke from her heart. But as Christy tried to make sense of the whole jumbled weekend, all she got for her efforts was a headache. When she slipped into bed that night, she hoped for a calm week to work through all her thoughts and feelings. Of course it would be calm, she reminded herself. She was on restriction.

CHAPTER SEVEN

One Hedgehog and One Rabbit to Go

"Here it is, Christy!" Katie said, waving a newspaper in her hand. Her red hair swished as she marched over to the school lunch table where Christy had just settled herself.

Katie plopped down across from Christy and thrust the newspaper under her nose. "I hoped I'd find you here in our old spot. How's your first day back treating you?"

"All right. What's with the paper?"

"I found a job for you. You said at church your parents were making you find a job, and here's the perfect one. At the mall, even."

Christy silently read the ad Katie had circled. Looking up, she said, "At the pet store?"

"Yes! Don't you see? It says, 'Experience with animals.' You did grow up on the kind of farm that had animals, didn't you?"

"Most Wisconsin dairy farms come equipped with animals, yes," Christy answered.

"See? You're a natural! Call them after school. I'll bet they hire you over the phone." Katie opened her sack lunch, examined its contents, and said, "Did you get anything more exciting than peanut butter and jelly?"

"You can have my apple," Christy offered.

"No, thanks. I don't touch food unless it's from one of my four basic food groups—sugars, fats, preservatives, and artificial flavorings."

Christy laughed and realized she hadn't smiled in several days. She hadn't heard from Rick since Sunday's standoff with her dad at the screen door. Being so far away from him made everything gloomy.

After running the pet shop idea past her mom, Christy called the number. The manager sounded young and in a hurry. He asked her to come in to fill out an application and then asked if she had reliable transportation and could work Friday nights. She said yes to both questions.

"Would it be possible for you to start this Friday?" he asked.

Remembering the restriction, she said, "I think so. I'll have to check and call you back."

"If you could come in around 7:00 tonight, you could fill out the application and give me your answer then."

"Okay. Thanks." Christy hung up, and turning to Mom said, "I think they might hire me. I'm supposed to go there tonight at 7:00. Is that okay?"

"I suppose. We'll ask your father when he comes home. He's still quite serious about your restriction."

"I know, but he was serious about a job, too. If I don't go in, they might hire somebody else."

Without much discussion, Christy's dad agreed to take her to the mall.

Before they walked into the pet store, her dad said, "Remember to stand up straight, speak clearly, and pretend I'm not here."

The first two instructions she could follow easily enough, but pretending Dad wasn't there would be impossible.

This is so embarrassing, she thought as she stepped up to the counter. *Suppose they find out he's with me? They might not hire me.*

"May I help you?" asked a guy behind the counter. He looked as though he was in his late twenties and had a rugged, earthy appearance. He wore his thick, black hair pulled back in a ponytail, which Christy was used to seeing on guys in California. But she was surprised that his ponytail was fastened with the type of plain green twist-tie usually found around celery stalks in the grocery store.

"I called this afternoon about the job, and Jon told me to come in and fill out an application."

"Oh, good. I'm Jon, and you're Christy, right?" He seemed surprised at her appearance. She knew it must be the dress. Mom insisted she wear a dress to make a favorable impression. Standing beside the myna birds, Christy felt like someone applying for a job to serve tea, not sell kitty litter.

"You can come in the back and fill out the paperwork. Do you know your social security number?" Jon asked, leading her past the tropical fish tanks to a card table in the back room.

"No, I don't think so."

"That's all right, as long as you bring it with you on your first day." He left her alone at the table with a one-page questionnaire and a pen.

Christy nervously answered the questions, remembering how Mom told her to use her best printing. Aside from her name, address, age, and phone number, she couldn't fill out much, since the other blanks related to previous job experience. The paper looked awfully empty. Christy decided to write in "baby-sitting" and left it at that.

As soon as she emerged from the back room, she saw her dad, pretending to look at the tropical fish. Hoping he wouldn't act as if he knew her, Christy walked straight to the front counter, bravely handing Jon her application.

"Baby-sitting, huh?" Jon said, scanning the paper. "And you said you lived on a farm?"

"Yes. In Wisconsin. For 14 years."

"And you're 16 now, I see." He then put the application down on the counter and rang up a customer's purchase on the cash register.

Christy smiled politely at the older couple, who were buying a blue jewel-studded cat collar. The couple smiled back, accepted their bag from Jon, and left.

"So, you haven't had any experience on a cash register."

Still smiling, Christy shook her head.

"Doesn't really matter. It's all computerized. You have to know how to read and push a few buttons. That's all. Computer does all the thinking." Jon turned the application over and wrote on the back as he verified, "You can work Fridays from 4:00 to 9:00, right? How about Saturdays, 11:00 to 6:00?"

"Sure, that would be fine," Christy said.

"Great!" Jon replied. "I'll see you Friday at 4:00. Oh, and you might be more comfortable wearing jeans to work. We don't tend to dress up much around here. The last girl who wore a flowered dress found the bunny rabbits nibbling on it. They thought she was a walking garden."

Christy smiled, said, "Okay, thanks," and left quickly to hide her embarrassment over her dress. Dad followed her out and acted proud of her. His affirmations helped make up for the insecurities she suddenly felt when she realized she had just been hired for her first job.

"What did I tell you?" Katie said the next day at school. "I knew the job was perfect for you. They don't get too many people with animal experience around here who are willing to work weekends for minimum wage."

"Oh, good! That makes me feel as if I'm the only one dumb enough to take this job," Christy said.

"I'm only kidding! You'll do great. It'll probably be a really fun job. I'll come see you, and you can sell me a dog bone or something. So when do you get off work?"

"At 9:00. Then I have to head straight home because of restriction," Christy said.

"Well," Katie sighed, "I hope you and Rick learn a lesson from all this. Now I guess we'll have to postpone our annual slumber party for two more weeks until your restriction is over."

"Where's it going to be?" Christy asked, remembering the back-to-school slumber party of last year. That night the girls had toilet-papered Rick's house. Since she had been the new girl at school, she hadn't a clue as to who Rick was. That's how she first met him.

All the girls had left her hiding in the bushes, and when Rick came out to clean up the paper, Christy had jumped out of the bushes and charged down the street with Rick running after her. The girls had returned in a motor home to pick her up, and Christy had hopped into the vehicle before Rick had a chance to catch her.

"Hello," Katie said, waving her hand in front of Christy's eyes. "Where did you just go?"

"Oh, I was remembering the slumber party last year. That was a wild night!"

"It sure was." Katie joined in the memory.

"Remember how Rick kept asking you who I was?" Christy said.

"I remember. He's been chasing you for a whole year. He must be pretty pleased with himself for finally catching you."

"What's that supposed to mean?" Christy asked.

"Well, if you want my opinion, Rick is the ultimate competitor. Remember the awards assembly when he graduated? He won an award in almost every athletic category."

"So? He likes sports," Christy said.

"He likes a challenge," Katie returned. "And you have been the ultimate challenge. You're about the only thing he didn't win while he was going to Kelley High."

"Oh, come on, Katie. You're exaggerating. Rick is a great guy, and I feel honored he wants me to be his girlfriend."

Katie shook her head, and a smirk crossed her face.

"What?" Christy asked. "What are you thinking?"

The bell rang, its annoying blare ending lunch and their discussion.

Katie hopped up from the table and replied, "You've changed, Christy. Six months ago you never would have said those words. But, hey, we all change. It's okay. I'll see you after school—at your new job."

Katie hurried off in the direction of the gym, leaving Christy to ponder their conversation as she walked to class.

We all change. We do. So what if I changed my opinion about Rick? I'm not doing anything wrong. Why can't a girl have a little fun without all her friends and relatives trying to make her feel bad? They're not giving me a chance, and they're really not giving Rick a chance.

Katie kept her word and showed up at the pet store a few minutes after Christy started work. Christy was standing at the register, and Jon was explaining how to run the computerized marvel. Christy didn't want to get in trouble her first day for having friends come in and distract her, so she acted as though she didn't see Katie come in.

"Pardon me," Katie said, acting out the part of a nonchalant customer. "Where do you keep your dog bones?"

Christy tightly pressed her lips together to keep from laughing.

"Second aisle, toward the back," Jon answered routinely and then finished drilling Christy on the register functions.

Christy remembered almost everything Jon showed her and answered five of his six questions correctly.

Katie approached the counter with two dog bones in her hands and said, "Excuse me. We have a poodle, and I was wondering if you could tell me which one of these he would like best."

It took a tremendous amount of self-control for Christy to not blow the role-playing. Katie seemed to have no problem keeping a straight face.

"Which one would you recommend, Christy?" Jon asked, turning the scenario over to her.

She cleared her throat twice before answering, "Probably the larger one."

"Fine," Katie said brightly. "Then I'll take the smaller one." She pulled a five-dollar bill out of her pocket and handed it to Christy.

Christy looked to Jon, and he said, "Go ahead. Remember which button you press first?"

Christy remembered. She tried to ignore Katie and think through each step on the cash register. It worked. The drawer opened when it was supposed to, and the screen displayed the correct amount of change due, which she handed to Katie without looking her in the eye.

"You'll do fine up here, Christy," Jon said. "I'm going in the back. If you need me, press this button." Jon showed her a red button under the counter.

The instant he was out of view, Christy let her facial muscles relax and said, "You almost got me fired!"

Katie giggled. "You know what? I changed my mind. Could I exchange this dog bone?"

"Not a chance. I have no idea how to do returns. Go find yourself a dog and give him a treat," Christy teased.

"Speaking of dogs," Katie retorted mischievously, "what's happening with Rick?"

"Katie, that was low!" Christy could feel her resentful thoughts from their lunch conversation returning. Katie had no right to be so critical of Rick.

"You know I'm only kidding. Is he coming in to see you tonight?"

"I don't know," Christy answered abruptly. Then she added, "Probably. I wrote him and told him about the job and everything." She felt like adding, "What do you care?" But she noticed Jon coming back up to the front.

He stepped behind the counter and pulled out a clipboard with a stack of papers attached to it. Noticing Katie still standing there, he said, "Is there a problem here?"

I'll say! Christy felt like answering. *My closest friend is acting like anything but a friend.*

"Yes, I changed my mind," Katie said, falling back into her role-playing voice. "I don't think Poopsie will like this bone. I'd like my money back."

Jon calmly put down the clipboard and said, "Watch, Christy. This is how you do a return."

He went through a few simple steps, and when the drawer opened, he asked Christy to count out the money and hand it back to the customer.

"Thank you," Katie said, smiling at Jon. "Your salesclerk here has been most helpful. I'll be sure to tell all my friends to shop here."

As soon as she walked out of the store, Jon said, "I hope her friends aren't like her."

Christy kept a straight face. After all, Katie deserved that comment.

"Come on back, and I'll show you how to clean the cages. Beverly," Jon called to the other salesclerk, who was stocking fish food, "will you cover the register?"

For the next half hour, Christy was tutored in the fine science of replacing shredded newspapers on the bottom of a wide variety of cages.

By the fifth cage, she thought, *Living on a farm didn't prepare me for this. Now, if I'd lived on Noah's ark, maybe.*

She then learned how to stock shelves, the right way to scoop up fish in a net, and which brand of dog food was on special. Jon didn't let up in his rapid training of every facet of the store, so Christy stopped him to ask questions. Twice she asked him to repeat his instructions because there were too many details to remember the first time through.

"Don't worry. You'll catch on," Jon said. "The last thing I need to show you is the snake."

Christy made a grim face. "As long as I don't have to touch it, I'll be fine."

Jon laughed at her squeamish response. "Walter wouldn't hurt a fly. A couple of rodents, or a small rabbit, yes. But not a fly." He smiled at his own joke. "Walter's over here in this locked terrarium."

Christy stood back as Jon showed her how to lock and unlock the tank of the 15-foot python. She nodded every time he looked at her to make sure she was taking in all the instructions.

"I won't ever have to feed him, though, will I?"

"Naw. I'm the only one who feeds him. I want you to keep an eye on this lock, though. It's an old tank and sometimes kids sneak back here and yank on the lock. They think it's funny to get Walter all excited."

Jon checked his watch. "Why don't you take a 15-minute break? When you come back, I have a dinner appointment."

Christy decided to spend her 15 minutes out in the mall rather than at the card table in the back room. As soon as she stepped into the open space, she noticed how good the air smelled. Sniffing her T-shirt, she realized she had brought the heavy odor of the menagerie with her.

Maybe I should visit a department-store perfume counter and sample a few perfumes?

"Going somewhere without me?" a deep voice behind Christy asked.

She spun around and met Rick's overpowering hug.

"Hi. I'm so glad to see you!" She squeezed his middle, then pulled back with a warning. "Better not get too close. I smell like a pet store."

"You smell fine," Rick said, leading her over to a bench. "What time do you get off?"

"Nine. I'm on a 15-minute break now. What's wrong? You look upset."

"Are you planning to work every Friday?"

"At first, yeah. That's the time they needed somebody. It might change later. Why?"

"Didn't you happen to think we might have plans for Friday nights?" Rick didn't try to conceal his anger. "There're plenty of jobs that need after-school help, Christy. You sure weren't think-ing when you took this one. Now all our Friday nights are shot."

"Rick, I'm sorry. I had to find a job, and this one came up, and—"

"And I suppose it's the only one you applied for. Man, Christy! I can't believe you did this. I mean, don't you think it would've been considerate of you to at least talk this over with me?"

Christy couldn't answer. Now she was afraid to tell him she also worked until 6:00 on Saturdays.

Why didn't I think of this before? I can't believe he's so mad at me!

"You know, this is great. I come home for the weekend, knowing that my girlfriend has been grounded because of some stupid thing about not calling to let her parents know I was driving her home. I can't talk to you all week, and your dad won't let up an inch. And now you're working every Friday night. That stinks, Christy! This is not the way to start off our relationship."

"I know," Christy whispered, feeling the tears bubbling up and spilling over onto her cheeks. "I'm sorry. I'll see if I can switch to another night."

"Why are you crying?" Rick slipped his arm around her and pulled her close. "Hey, it'll all work out. It took me by surprise, that's all. You'll be able to switch your hours or get another job or something."

He held her for a few minutes while she dried her tears.

"I'm sorry," Christy said, "but I probably should get back. I was only supposed to be gone 15 minutes."

"You still have a few minutes," Rick said, stroking her hair. "I haven't had a chance to tell you how much I missed you this week. I thought about you every day."

"I missed you, too," Christy said. "I'm glad you're here." She smiled and wiped away one last tear. "Is my face okay?" she asked.

"Your face is great," he said, smiling broadly.

"You know what I mean. Did I smear my makeup?"

"A tiny bit, right here." Rick stroked his thumb under her left eye. "There, Killer Eyes. Now you're perfect."

"Far from it," Christy retorted.

"For me, you're perfect. Come on. I'll walk you back, and you can introduce me to all the animals. Except your manager. I've already met him."

"Jon is nice," Christy said defensively.

"I'm sure he is. If you like the zookeeper type. You don't, do you? I mean, he's not asking you out or anything?"

"Rick!" Christy playfully socked him in the arm as they entered the pet store.

"Just checking. Can't say I was too worried about competing with Tarzan, though."

Jon more than likely overheard Rick's last comment as they walked in because he gave Rick and Christy a scowl. Rick took off toward the back, where they kept the tropical fish. Christy stepped behind the counter, and Jon pointed at the clock on the wall behind him. "You left at 5:30, Christy."

She looked up at the clock. It was now five minutes after 6:00. "Is that clock right? I couldn't have been gone that long! It seemed like only a few minutes. I'm sorry. I won't let it happen again."

"Good. I'm taking your word on that. I'm late for an appointment. I won't be back until 7:30. Beverly is in the back; she can help out if you get stuck on anything."

"Sure. Thanks. And again, I'm really sorry about losing track of the time."

Jon lifted a hand in a slight wave over his shoulder as he rushed off. Christy felt relieved that Jon had been so understanding. She promised herself she'd never let herself be late again. That would be so unfair, especially when Jon had let it go this time.

A young boy with his mother passed Jon on his way out. They came right to the counter, and the boy said, "I want to buy a hedgehog, and it has to be a boy."

"We need some help," the mother said sweetly.

"Sure," Christy said, pushing the buzzer, which she hoped would produce Beverly. "We'll be with you in a moment."

Another boy now stood before her with a packaged aquarium filter in his hand and asked, "Do you know if this comes with the charcoal, or do I have to buy that separately?"

"Um, I'm not sure. Does it say on the package?"

The boy scanned the package, and Christy rang the buzzer again. Down the aisle trotted Beverly. With her long black hair in a single braid down her back, and her wrists covered with beaded bracelets, Beverly looked like the kind of young woman who, if she had lived a hundred years ago, would have been a Pony Express rider.

Christy explained what each customer wanted, and Beverly said, "I'll take care of the register. You go on back and show them the hedgehogs. And no, the charcoal is separate. It's at the end of the far right aisle."

"The hedgehogs are back here," Christy said, trying to sound as if she knew what she was doing.

Maybe I'll be able to figure out which are the boys if I pick up a couple of them and check them out inconspicuously.

"I want that one," the boy said when they stopped in front of the cage with the African Pygmy hedgehogs.

"Does he roll up into a ball? I only want the kind that can roll up into a ball and eats bugs. I'm gonna name him Sonic. He'd better be a boy."

Christy and the mother exchanged knowing glances, and Christy said, "My little brother is 10. He's hedgehog crazy, too."

She gingerly picked up the hedgehog, and its pointy spines pricked her hand. She tried to check the underside to see if it was a boy, but it instantly rolled up into a little ball. Putting the spiny creature down and pulling out another one, she tried to get it to open up so she could figure out if it was a boy or a girl.

"You have to get it to relax," Rick said, reaching for the hedgehog.

Christy didn't know how long he'd been standing there watching her.

"You can tell by the location of the belly button," Rick said as he soothingly coaxed it to open up. "The ones with the higher belly buttons are boys."

"You're kidding," Christy said. "I mean, yes. Right. Thanks."

"Yes, thank you," the mother said, smiling at Rick.

"You want this one," Rick said.

"Can you show us what we need to feed him, and how big of a tank we should buy?"

"No problem," Rick volunteered, leading the three of them around the store, collecting a tank and lid, food and water dishes, and wood shavings for bedding. "They like little tunnels to hide in. I think there're some plastic ones over here."

Christy caught Rick's proud glance as he pointed out the best kind of tunnels. He threw in a couple of pointers on feeding Sonic primarily cat food but throwing in an occasional mealworm or cricket as a tasty treat every now and then.

With their arms loaded, the mom and her son laid out their extensive purchases on the counter. Beverly's eyebrows arched slightly on her plain face, and she said, "I guess you figured out which one was a boy."

"I had a little help," Christy explained, sneaking a wink at Rick, who had retreated to the bird-food section only a few feet away. He puffed out his chest jokingly and winked back.

Beverly returned to her inventory labeling in the back while Christy rang up the $205 hedgehog sale.

The woman handed Christy her check and said, "Won't my husband be surprised! I'm sure I'll hear about when he was a kid, and they fished their pets right out of the creek for free."

Rick strutted his way to the counter when the mom and son left and said, "Bring on the next customer. They can't resist, can they?"

Before Christy had a chance to swat at him for his joking arrogance, a man came up and said, "Can you answer some questions about the rabbits?"

"Sure," Rick said. "Let me help you." He followed the man back to the cages. Twenty minutes later Christy rang up a $184 rabbit sale.

"You'd better leave before Jon comes back," Christy said, checking the clock and noticing it was nearly 7:30.

"Why? I'm making money for the guy. He should put me on the payroll!" Rick grinned and then said, "Don't worry. I'll disappear. Actually, I ordered something, and I want to see if it's ready. I'll be back at 9:00 to pick you up."

"I drove my car here," Christy said.

"You still need a bodyguard to walk you through the parking lot. I'll see you at 9:00." He waved and took off.

Not a minute too soon. Jon came in from the opposite direction only a few seconds later.

"How did it go? Any problems?" he asked.

"No, not really," Christy said as Jon reached around and did a subtotal check on the cash register.

"This can't be right. It says you did more than $400 in sales while I was gone. What did you sell?"

"Just a hedgehog and a rabbit," Christy said with a smile. "And all the accessories they needed plus a month's food supply."

"Really?" Jon said. "How 'bout that. Guess I did the right thing hiring you. Keep up the good work!"

CHAPTER EIGHT

Number Eight on the List

"Come here, girlfriend," Rick said in the mall parking lot after he had walked Christy to her car. "I've waited all week to give you this."

He opened his arms and wrapped Christy in a warm hug. "Sorry about getting mad earlier. It won't be so bad spending a few Friday nights helping you sell out the store. And once you're off restriction, we can still take in a late movie."

Christy pulled back from his soft voice in her ear and decided to let him have all the bad news at one time. "Rick, even after I'm off restriction, I still have to be home by 10:00. And I didn't get a chance to talk to Jon about changing my hours. I'm also scheduled for 11:00 to 6:00 on Saturdays."

Rick released his hold and looked at her in disbelief. "You agreed to work Saturdays, too? All day? What were you thinking, Christy?"

"I needed the job. I told you that."

"Fine, fine!" Rick said, holding up his hands as though he didn't want to touch this topic any longer. "You go ahead and have your job and have your two weeks' restriction. That should give you enough time to figure out where I fit in your life. I've waited too long for us to be together to end up jumping all these hurdles you keep putting in my way."

"Rick . . . ," Christy began, trying to reason with him, but he'd already stalked off, leaving her alone by her car.

She drove home, refusing to cry, and went right to bed. What a mess her life had turned into.

The next morning she showed up at work at 10:30, hoping her early arrival would help make up for the extended break the night before.

"Good morning, Jon," she said cheerfully. She had on some of the new clothes Marti had bought her—shorts and a flowered T-shirt. She had taken extra care with her hair and makeup, hoping Rick would come in to see her and that his anger would have evaporated.

"Check out the delivery that came in this morning," Jon said, motioning toward the back.

Christy found a large wire cage on the floor in the back room holding three adorable cocker spaniel puppies. She unlatched the door and reached for the one with the caramel-colored fur. He eagerly tried to lick her face while his flying tail beat the air like a high-speed wire whisk.

"You are the cutest little thing I've ever seen!" she said. "You look exactly like our old dog, Taffy."

"You had a cocker?" Jon asked.

"When I was a kid. She was the sweetest dog. She used to run between the cows' legs when they were being milked. It's a miracle she never was kicked."

"These three are all males. They have their papers, and they should sell pretty fast. Why don't you get the front window ready for them?"

Christy went to work, preparing the front window case for the puppies and scooting them into the display one by one. They drew a crowd right away, and Christy's favorite one sold before noon.

"You take good care of this puppy, okay?" Christy said to the little girl squirming with glee as her dad attached the collar and leash. "I had a puppy just like this when I was your age."

"What did you name him?" the girl asked, with a grin that revealed a gap where her two front teeth had been.

"Taffy, because our dog was this color, too, and we thought she looked like taffy."

"Can we name our dog Taffy? Please, Daddy? Could we?"

"Whatever you want, Rachel," the dad said, smiling his approval. "He's all yours now."

"Come here, Taffy," she called, patting her open palms on her thighs. "Come here."

The cocker jumped up and licked her face before the dad tugged on the leash to get him down.

"He likes me, Daddy!" she squealed. "Taffy likes me. Come on, Taffy."

They made a cute procession—the little girl running ahead, patting her legs, and calling out "Taffy" as the dog scampered toward her, pulling the dad with him.

"Another satisfied customer, I see," Jon said, checking the register's subtotal. "Looks good," he noted, reading the figures. "Why don't you stay on the register until Beverly comes back from lunch, and then it'll be your turn to go."

It seemed the customers came in nonstop. All the business helped Christy keep her mind off Rick.

But during her lunch hour, the loneliness crept back. She went to the mall food court and stood in line to buy a corn dog and lemonade. While she ate, she kept looking around, hoping to see

Rick. She saw some girls from school and a family from church, but no Rick.

The rest of the afternoon went by more slowly. When work ended at 6:00, she felt tired and discouraged.

After dinner Mom reminded her it was her turn to do the dishes and fold the laundry. Christy completed her chores silently and with a sour attitude.

Finally, at 8:00 she had time to herself. She rummaged around in her room for a packet of Victorian Rose bath powder and treated herself to a long, luxurious soak in the tub.

Life is so brutal, she thought, rubbing the animal smells off her tired arms. *Men are so strange. In some ways I wish my parents wouldn't have let me date until I turned 17. No, 18. My life was so much simpler before I could drive and date. It's terrible being allowed do both at the same age. Only one more week of restriction, and then, when Rick and I date again, hopefully things will be okay with us. We can start fresh. Everything can be dazzling again.*

The next week seemed gobbled up by the homework monster. Christy's junior year was definitely going to be harder than her sophomore year. Thursday night she stayed up until 11:00, reading for her literature class.

At last she crumpled into bed, thinking, *I wish Rick could have called this week—even though I don't know when I would have had the time to talk to him. I miss him so much. I hope he comes to work tomorrow night.*

By 4:00 Friday afternoon, the last thing Christy wanted to do was go to work. She felt exhausted and wished she could just take a nap. Having slept too late that morning, she hadn't had time to wash her hair and had pulled it back in a ponytail with a white scrunchie. Her white, embroidered cotton shirt got a stain on it at lunch when she spilled some orange juice down the front. She wished she had time to go home and change.

Few customers came to the pet store, so Jon had Christy work in the back, marking prices on cans of cat food. She didn't mind, since she was able to sit on the floor while she worked. But it concerned her that she was hidden from view and wouldn't be able to spot Rick if he came by.

During her break, she sat out in front of the shop and ate a granola bar from the health food store next door. Rick never showed up.

Am I crazy, sitting around waiting for Rick like this? Katie was right. Six months ago, I never would have done this. What changed in me? Whatever it was, I'm not sure I like it. I don't think I've ever felt this lonely or depressed before in my life. I wonder if Rick misses me, too, or if he's getting into college life and isn't even thinking about me.

The Saturday shift turned out to be a repeat of the previous Saturday—busy all day. Christy consoled herself by thinking that Rick probably hadn't come home from college that weekend, since he knew she would still be on restriction. Tomorrow restriction would end, and then everything would change.

Monday afternoon Rick called about five minutes after she walked in the door from school.

"You're off restriction, right?" were his first words.

"Rick!" Christy headed straight for her bedroom and lowered her voice. "I've missed you so much!"

"I can take care of that. Do I have clearance from headquarters to come over?"

"Now? Where are you?"

"About three blocks away. I tried to catch you at school, but I wasn't fast enough."

"Hang on a minute. I'll ask my mom if it's okay." Christy left the phone in her room and approached Mom cautiously. "Rick's

on the phone. Would it be all right if he came over? I'm off restriction, and I don't have much homework. Could he even stay
for dinner, maybe?"

"I suppose it would be all right. We're having spaghetti for
dinner. Nothing fancy. Does he like spaghetti?"

"Rick *loves* Italian food. Thanks, Mom!" Christy felt as if she
were flying as she raced back to her room to retrieve the phone.
"Sure, Rick. My mom said that would be fine. And can you stay
for dinner?"

"Probably not. I have a 7:00 class tonight, so I'll have to leave
by 5:30 to make it back in time. I'll be right over."

"I'll see you in a few minutes," she said, hanging up and racing to her closet. She changed into her favorite pair of shorts and
a clean T-shirt. It wasn't her nicest outfit, but it was definitely her
most comfortable.

With lightning speed, she did a quick fix on her makeup and
hair. *Rick, if I'd known you were coming, I would have spent a lot more
time on my hair this morning. Look at me! I'm just thrown together. I
look awful! Maybe I should change. These shorts are really old.*

"Christy," Mom called through the bathroom door, "Rick's
here."

"I'll be right there." She decided to go as she was and grabbed
some perfume from the basket on the counter, then stopped before giving herself a squirt. It was a new bottle of Amazon Gardenia. She used to wear it around Todd, and he had said it reminded him of Hawaii. No, she definitely could not wear Amazon
Gardenia with Rick. Scrounging in the bottom of her makeup
bag, she found a tiny sample she had picked up some time ago at
the mall. Snapping open the vial, Christy rubbed the heavy,
musky fragrance onto her wrists. *Phew! What is this stuff? It's not
me at all.*

Anxiously trying to dab it off with a tissue, Christy gave up. *I don't want to make Rick mad by having him wait too long. I'll have to go like this. My hair is a disaster!*

With her heart pounding but a wide smile on her face, Christy made her entrance into the living room. Rick rose from the couch when he saw her and gave one of his "I bet you're glad to see me" grins.

Did Christy notice a slight twinge of disappointment on his face? Was it because of what she had on? Her hair? She scolded herself for being so paranoid and said, "Would you like something to drink, Rick?"

"No, actually, I was planning on making a run to 7-Eleven. I already asked your mom, and she said it was fine for us to go as long as I had you back in time for dinner. Shall we?" he asked, offering her his arm and escorting her to the car.

When they pulled into the 7-Eleven parking lot, Christy recognized eight guys out front who were sitting on the hoods of their cars. They were all on the football team and old buddies of Rick's.

Christy felt self-conscious and out of place as the casual introductions were made. The guys all started to joke and talk about things that made no sense to Christy. She was the only girl there.

After about five minutes, Rick pulled some money out of his pocket and turning to Christy, he said, "You want to go buy me a Big Gulp? Cherry Coke."

What else could she do? Christy took the money and stood in line to buy Rick's Cherry Coke. She felt funny about getting anything for herself, so she didn't. For another half hour they stood by the cars out front. Christy said a total of about seven words. Rick's friends treated her as if she were a nameless, personality-less, devoted admirer of his. Last year at school she had avoided this group like the flu. Now she was stuck in the middle of them.

"We have to go," Rick suddenly announced, tossing his cup into the trash and making a perfect shot. "Two points," he said. "See you guys around."

"Bye," Christy said meekly and followed Rick to the car.

"How was your week?" Christy asked, anxious to turn the conversation in her direction after being ignored for so long. "How's school going?"

"Good."

"Do you like your classes and everything?" she ventured, hoping for a more detailed answer.

Rick turned a corner sharply, causing his wheels to squeal. "You sound like my mother, Christy."

"I'm sorry. I've been thinking about you all week and wondered how you were doing, that's all."

"I've been thinking about you, too. That's why I came all the way up here this afternoon. I've missed you."

Turning another corner, Rick stopped by a park and turned off the engine.

"Here we are," he said. "We're going to do number eight on my date list. Play on the swings at the park."

He jogged around, opened her door, and escorted her to the children's play area.

"Rick, this is crazy!" Christy said, noticing five or six children on the swings. "We can't take the swings away from those little kids."

"Hey, I'm not going to bully them. We'll wait our turn. Look. The merry-go-round is open. Come on, I'll give you a spin."

Those zany, dazzling feelings were beginning to return to

Christy. She jumped on the merry-go-round, held tight, and teased, "Don't go too fast."

"Don't worry," Rick said. "I'll go really slow. Slow as a snail."

Before he had finished his last word, Rick grabbed the metal bar and took off running a tight circle in the sand.

Christy laughed into the wind and called out, "Not so fast!"

Three kids suddenly appeared. "Let us on!" they cried. "Stop. We want a ride."

Rick obliged, bringing the spinning merry-go-round to a halt. Christy took advantage of the opportunity to hop off while the little kids climbed on. She stepped back a few feet, brushing her hair out of her face, and admired Rick's playful nature with the screaming kids as he spun them around and around.

That's my boyfriend. Look at him. What a great guy, playing with the kids like that. Why is it I can feel both wonderful and terrible around him in such a short time? Does he have any idea how much control he has over my feelings?

Christy noticed that the swings were now empty. She positioned herself in the middle one, facing Rick. Slowly she swayed back and forth, watching him and listening to the happy sounds emerging from his spinning fan club.

The September afternoon was clear and sunny, still warm but with a soft breeze blowing in from the ocean, which was about 15 miles west of them. Fall was tiptoeing in on ballet slippers, trying not to disturb the last few days of summer. Even the air already smelled like autumn to Christy.

Rick left the merry-go-round and the band of dizzy riders and walked toward Christy. With his hand clutching his chest, he said, "That's my workout for the day."

"You're not done yet," Christy said playfully. "You still have to push me in the swing. Remember? Number eight on your list?"

Rick came around behind her and clutched the two long chains in his strong arms. "Okay, baby. You asked for it!" He drew her back like a human arrow in a bow and let her go.

"Whoa!" she shrieked, holding on and feeling herself take flight.

Rick's push turned gentle when her swing returned to him. He pressed his hands against her back, and Christy stretched her legs out in front of her, pointing her toes toward the blue sky.

She felt silly and carefree. This is how she always imagined it would be to have a boyfriend, and this is how she wanted it to always be with Rick. Feeling happy and having fun like this was so much better than the gloom and depression she had battled all week when she wasn't with him.

"This is so much fun, Rick!" she called over her shoulder. "I haven't been on a swing for ages."

"Neither have I," Rick said, leaving his post and confiscating the vacant swing next to her. "Let's have a race."

They both pushed toward the sky, higher and higher, laughing and shouting like kids. Christy's swing chain began to tug and jerk each time she went up.

She slowed down and said, "Okay, okay, you win."

"As usual," Rick said, slowing to keep pace with her back-to-earth level. "I moved into the apartment with Doug and two other guys."

"Really? How's that working out?" Christy asked as they slowly swung back and forth and caught their breath.

"Okay. Beats the dorms any day. None of us knows how to cook, and we're pretty low on furniture. Other than that, it's fine."

Christy still didn't know how she felt about Rick slipping so easily into Doug's life and taking Todd's place in some ways.

"You haven't told me yet what you've decided," Rick said.

"About what?"

"About work. Have you changed your hours yet?"

Christy swallowed and hoped her answer would satisfy him. "I have to stay on Fridays for at least another month. There's another girl who said she'd work my Saturdays whenever I wanted, because she needs the extra money. I can't give up too many Saturdays, though, because I wouldn't be getting paid enough."

Rick stopped his swing and sat still, kicking the sand. "I had plans for us for this weekend. I guess it means more to me than it does to you for us to be together."

"I can get off this Saturday. What were your plans?" His pouting made her more irritated than nervous.

"Never mind," he said.

"Rick, I'm doing the best I can!" Christy spouted. "Give me a chance. I can get off Saturday, my restriction is over, and I'm as anxious as you are to spend time together. So, come on. Let's work it out."

"All right, let's try this. I wanted to fly kites at the beach, have Mexican food in Carlsbad, and then go to the movies. Think we can do all that, or do you have time limits on your dates?"

"No, of course not. It sounds great. I'll clear everything and let you know as soon as I find out, okay?"

"It's okay for me to start calling you?" Rick asked.

"Yes." Christy felt that everything was going to work out, and already she was eager to spend Saturday with Rick.

"One more race," Rick challenged, kicking off and pushing his swing into high gear.

Christy followed his lead, pointing her toes toward the sky and trying to swing high enough to keep up with her boyfriend.

CHAPTER NINE

Where's Walter?

After Rick dropped her off, Christy made a few phone calls and arranged to take off from work on Saturday. At dinner, she approached the plan carefully with her parents.

"I don't like the idea of your starting to take off work already," Dad said. "It's okay this time, but I don't think you should do it again except if you're sick or we have something planned as a family."

"It's okay with you, though, if Rick and I spend Saturday together? Going to the beach, dinner in Carlsbad, and to a movie?" Christy wanted to make sure no glitches existed in her weekend plans.

Her mom and dad exchanged glances. "As long as you're back by 10:00, it's okay. We're strict about curfew, though. One minute past 10:00, and you're back on restriction," Dad said.

Christy felt certain they could have an early dinner and find a movie that ended before 10:00. She couldn't wait to tell Rick everything was clear.

He called the next day after school, and when she told him, he sounded pleased. She felt great.

"I have a surprise for you," Rick said.

"Oh, really? What?"

"You'll find out Saturday."

"Can I try to guess?" Christy asked.

"You can try, but it won't do you any good. You'll never guess. You might as well wait and be surprised."

They talked for more than an hour, and then it was time for dinner. Christy moaned when she realized it was her turn to do dishes again. She had let some of her homework from the previous night slide because of spending the afternoon with Rick at the park and being too tired to stay up much past 9:00. So tonight she had an abundance of reading to do.

It was nearly 10:30 when Christy decided she couldn't keep her eyes open any longer. She still had four chapters to read and two pages of math. She gave up and went to sleep.

The next morning she felt awful. All day she seemed to be dragging.

At lunch Katie started in with her advice. "If you ask my opinion, you're coming down with something. You have that red look around the eyes."

Things had been tense between them for the past few days, and Katie's comments about how Christy looked didn't help much. Christy had learned to keep their conversations on neutral subjects, like school.

"That's from reading so much," she said. "And I didn't even come close to finishing it all last night. What is with all the homework this year?"

"They're getting us ready for college, didn't you know?" Katie bit into a candy bar. "Have you picked out your poem yet for literature class?"

"No. Have you?"

"I think so. They're all pretty hard to read aloud because of all the *thee*s and *thou*s. I mean, if we're supposed to stand up in front of the class and read one of these romantic masterpieces, you'd think they'd at least give us some written in English."

"They are in English, Katie. Victorian English. That's why they're from the Victorian poetry section, remember?" Christy didn't feel like eating much. This was one of the last warm Indian-summer days, and all she wanted to do was stretch out in the shade and sleep.

"Well, let me know what poem you pick and tell me if it's easy," Katie said.

Christy stopped by the library on the way home and found a book with some of the suggested poems for class. She checked out the book, went right home, and took a nap. Mom woke her in time for dinner, which Christy ate little of.

"Are you feeling okay, Christy? Do you think you're coming down with something?" Mom asked, placing her cool hand on Christy's forehead.

The hand on the forehead reminded her of something. What was it? Todd. Todd's blessing that early morning on the beach.

That tiny memory acted like a key, unlocking a treasure chest of thoughts and feelings. Christy fought to keep it all shut up inside.

"I'm okay," she told her mom. "Just tired out from too much homework, I think. I have a bunch more tonight, too."

"I'll help you with the dishes," Mom offered.

They finished up by 7:15, but just as Christy was ready to plunge into the homework pool, Rick called. She curled up with the phone on the end of her bed and let his soothing voice erase her earlier flashes of Todd.

"I miss you," Rick said. "I've been counting the days until

Friday. You don't mind if I spend the evening at a certain pet store, do you?"

"As long as I don't get in trouble." Christy couldn't believe how energetic she began to feel as she talked to Rick.

"You know what I miss?" Rick asked. "I miss the smell of your hair."

"My hair? What does my hair smell like?"

"I don't know. It smells fresh, like lemons or something. And I miss the way your hand feels in mine—so soft and little."

Christy looked at her hands as he spoke his gentle words. She never had thought of them as little before. She noticed the nails were chipped on three of her fingers. She made a note to do her nails before Friday. Rick would notice.

He said a handful of sweet, heartwarming things he liked about Christy. When she hung up at 9:00, she felt like a princess who had just been thoroughly adored. She decided to put off her homework and work on her nails.

On Friday morning she was noticing a spot she had missed, when her literature teacher called out in class, "Christy Miller? Which poem have you selected to read in class next week?"

Christy grabbed the book she had checked out of the library. Quickly running her eyes down the list of Victorian poems, she stopped at one near the bottom of the page because it was written by someone who shared her first name.

"I'm going to read, 'Twice,' by Christina Rossetti," she answered. She hoped it was a short poem. Before she had a chance to look it up in the book, the bell rang.

"You didn't tell me you picked a poem," Katie said, joining Christy as they walked into the noisy hall.

"I didn't have one until a minute ago. I just picked it," she confessed. "Where did you find yours?"

"I went for one on the handout. The shortest one. Do you want to hear the first few lines? I have it right here. Tell me if this doesn't remind you of something." Katie held her paper up and read,

> I plucked pink blossoms from mine apple tree
> And wore them all that evening in my hair:
> Then in due season when I went to see
> I found no apples there.

Katie looked up at Christy, waiting for her response.

Christy shrugged her shoulders.

"Well?" Katie prodded. "Doesn't it make you think of something?"

"No. What's it supposed to make me think of?"

"Oh, nothing, I guess," Katie said, sticking the paper back in her folder. "Only it made me think of certain people who dance around with blossoms in their hair, not realizing there won't be any apples later."

"What are you trying to tell me?" Christy felt her anger begin to bubble up again. "This is about Rick, isn't it? You've been dying to give me your advice for weeks now. Why don't you get it over with? What do you have against him?"

Katie's face turned red. "You want to know what I think? Good! I'll tell you. You're making a mammoth mistake going out with him. Rick is bad news. He's going to break your heart. Why couldn't you have gone out with him once and left it at that? Why did you have to break up with Todd and chain yourself to Rick?"

"Katie, it's not like that. I explained all this to you already. I didn't plan on things happening this way. They just happened!"

"Yeah, well, if the blossoms fit, wear them. But don't expect me to feel sorry for you when they die and you discover there are no apples left on your tree!" With a swish of her red hair, Katie turned and marched off to class.

What was that supposed to mean? What's her problem?

Two classes later, Katie stood waiting for Christy at her locker. "I'm sorry," Katie said. "Are you still speaking to me?"

Christy considered snubbing her for an instant but realized this was her closest friend. She hated arguing with her.

"I just don't understand why you're so against Rick," Christy said, spinning through the combination on her lock. "You're not giving him a chance, and I don't think you're giving me a chance, either."

"I know. You're right."

"You don't know Rick like I do. He's a perfect gentleman to me. I'm having a hard enough time with my parents putting me on restriction and trying to get used to a new job, without my best friend yelling at me, too."

"You're right, Christy. I told you before that I supported you, and I want to. It's just hard because now that you're working and have a boyfriend, you don't seem to have much time left for me."

"Then we'll have to plan on doing something together. I'm not trying to ignore you."

"I know. You have a lot going on. I understand that. We'll have to figure out a time for our slumber party."

"Sure!" Christy agreed, feeling as though things had cleared up between them. "We still have to have our slumber party. Maybe next weekend."

"Okay," Katie agreed. "Next weekend. Definitely next weekend."

As Christy drove to work after school, she thought, *My life is getting so complex. All of a sudden I have no time to do the things I used to.*

She pulled into a gas station and prepared to pump nearly half of her first paycheck into the tank of the car she shared with her mom.

Yes, she sighed as the sickening smell of gasoline filled her nostrils, *life is certainly complex.*

She arrived at work five minutes late and explained to Jon, "I had to buy gas. Have you noticed how expensive gas is lately?"

"Actually, prices are down a little," he said. "Oh, by the way, your boyfriend came by."

Christy stopped and looked at Jon. "My boyfriend?"

How does he know about Rick? He was here only one time. What did Rick do, come in and bully Jon by saying, 'Stay away from her, Tarzan. She's mine'?

"Yeah, your boyfriend." Jon had a wry smile on his face, enjoying teasing her.

"Did he say anything?"

"No. He'll be back, though. He went into the jewelry store."

Christy was surprised at Jon's perceptiveness. "You don't miss a thing, do you?" she said, feeling free to tease him back a little.

"Nope, not a thing. Do you want to hear what your best friend looks like? You know, the redhead with the poodle named Poopsie?"

Now Christy felt embarrassed. How did Jon notice all these things?

"And I knew you were from a farm when I saw your dad."

"I can't believe you! Do you have radar tracking skills or something?" Christy said, wondering how many other nonchalant things she had done in the store, assuming he wasn't watching.

"After you work here awhile, you figure out different types of people. By the way, I have to leave early tonight, so Beverly is going to lock up. I know you're not working tomorrow, but I wanted to make sure you could stay a little after 9:00 tonight in case Beverly needs help closing."

"Okay, that's fine," Christy said.

"Good. Here comes your boyfriend. I'm leaving you at the register. I don't mind if you talk to him, as long as you don't neglect any of the customers. And as long as you don't get into any lovers' quarrels. Tends to be bad for attracting walk-in business." Jon smiled at his own dry humor and took off for the back of the store.

"Hi," Rick said. Checking to make sure no one else was around, he leaned over the counter and gave Christy a quick kiss on the cheek.

"Hi," Christy said, startled at his greeting.

"I have a surprise for you," Rick said. "But you don't get it until tomorrow. Think you can wait until then?"

"I guess. If I have to. Jon figured out that you were my boyfriend," she said. "He said he didn't mind if you hung out as long as it didn't keep me away from the customers."

"Oh, and did you happen to tell him what a wonderful salesperson I am?"

Christy giggled, remembering the night Rick sold the hedgehog and the rabbit. "No, but I'll be sure to mention it when the time is right. Why don't you find some poor, unsuspecting person and sell him one of the tropical birds tonight? Those are expensive. Or, I know, better yet, why don't you find a new home for Walter? Jon would love you forever."

"Who's Walter?" Rick asked.

"The snake back there. The huge, ugly, neglected one."

"And you're one of his biggest fans, I can tell," Rick teased. Then turning more serious, he said, "I won't be able to sell Walter for you tonight, babe. I'm going for pizza with some of the guys and then to the game. I only stopped by to tell you what time I'm picking you up in the morning."

Christy's heart sank. First she had to give up time with Katie because of her date with Rick, and now he was going to the football game while she worked.

Rick must have read the disappointment in her eyes because he said, "Hey, come on. We'll have all day together tomorrow, remember? I'm going to pick you up at 11:00, so be ready and bring a jacket."

"Okay," she answered, trying to look more cheerful. "I'll be thinking about you all night, though."

"You're not going to miss me a bit," Rick teased. "Not when you have Walter and Tarzan to keep you company." He checked again to see that no one was looking and gave her another quick kiss on the other cheek before jetting out the door.

Fortunately, it turned out to be a busy evening, and Christy didn't have much time to feel sorry for herself.

Jon left at 8:00, and Christy had customers at the register right up to 9:00. None of them was a big sale. Most were small things like fish food and dog bones. She couldn't figure out why on some days they had only a few customers, while on other days, like tonight, the store was packed with people.

At 9:00, Beverly took hold of the metal door that shut them off from the rest of the mall and pulled it halfway down. "We're closed!" she called to the three kids at the back of the store.

The kids scampered out, laughing and punching each other in the arms.

"A bunch of 10-year-old delinquents," Beverly muttered, closing the door the rest of the way. "Don't they have homes? Where are their parents?"

"Do you want me to do anything else?" Christy asked. "I ran a final total on the cash register and bundled all the checks."

"I can do the rest. Thanks."

Christy got her backpack and said good night.

"Before you go," Beverly called out, "could you check all the cages? Make sure all the critters are bedded down for the night."

"Sure," Christy called back. She checked all the birds, rabbits, kittens, and puppies. They were all fine. She did a quick check on the fish, lizards, and turtles and was ready to tell Beverly everything was okay, when she saw it.

Walter's cage was open, and Walter was gone.

"Bev-er-ly!" Christy yelled, scanning the floor. "Come here, quick!"

Christy ran for the back room and hopped up on a chair, which is where Beverly found her.

"It's Walter," Christy explained. "He's out of his cage."

"Oh no," Beverly groaned. "Now I know why those kids acted as though they had some big joke when they left. We have to find him before he slips through the door and gets loose in the mall."

Christy grabbed a broom that was propped up against the wall and cautiously came down from her chair. "You go first," she said.

Beverly stuck close beside her as they slowly made their way down each of the aisles.

"Here, Walter," Beverly called under her breath.

Christy couldn't tell if she was acting nervous or silly.

"Where would he go?" Christy asked.

"Just about anywhere. We probably should get on our hands and knees to look, because he likes tight, dark spots."

"Not me," Christy said. "There's no way I want to get on nose level with that monster."

Just then Walter shot out from under the bags of dog food and slithered under the cash register counter with a speed that surprised Christy.

She screamed, "Get him!" and held the broom over her head.

Beverly yelled, "Don't hit him. I'll try to corner him."

She bravely grabbed a trash can, dumped out its contents, and stepped behind the counter. "Here, Walter, Walter, Walter. Come here, boy."

They could hear a rustling noise like someone trying to open a bag of potato chips and squashing most of the contents in the attempt.

"Come on, Walter. We know you're here somewhere," Beverly said, her nervousness peeking through.

Christy cautiously moved back in case the villain decided to make a run for it in her direction. She scrambled on top of a stack of 50-pound bags of dog food, using the broom as a support.

All went completely quiet. Too quiet. The only sound was the gurgling of the fish tanks at the back.

"Where is he?" Christy whispered.

"He's not on this side. Can you see anything on your side?" Beverly asked.

Stretching her neck and leaning on her broom, Christy bent all the way forward to view the floor by the counter. It was too much strain for the bags of dog food, and the top bag began to slip. Christy tried to stop the landslide, but the broom bristles gave way to the sudden weight. She crashed to the floor, her arms and legs splayed in different directions, with chunks of dog food spilling from the torn bag and raining down her back.

"Are you all right?" Beverly ran over and grabbed Christy by the arm.

Christy groaned and opened her eyes. Then she froze.

Not more than two feet away lay the beast, as frozen as Christy was.

Beverly didn't see him. She continued her first aid survey. "Is anything broken? Can you move at all?"

Before Christy could breathe or even blink an eye, Walter turned and made a slithering getaway through the barred door and out into the mall. Beverly saw him make his escape.

"Oh no!" she said, jumping up and unlocking the door. "We have to get him!"

Christy, realizing her paralysis had come from fear, not broken vertebrae, pulled herself to her feet and numbly followed Beverly into the empty mall.

"Which way did he go?" Christy asked.

"This way. He's headed toward that big planter," Beverly said, running after him.

When they turned the corner, a security guard yelled out, "Halt right there!" He stood with his feet apart, his hand on his holster.

"It's okay!" Beverly yelled. "We work here. At the pet store. One of our animals escaped, that's all!"

The guard joined them by the planter and asked, "What's loose? One of those frisky rabbits?"

"Not exactly," Beverly said, looking at Christy and then back at the security guard. "It was Walter."

"Walter?" the guard said.

"You know, our 15-foot python. Walter." Beverly cautiously peered into the foliage.

"A snake? You two girls let a snake get out? I'm calling for backup." The guard whipped out his walkie-talkie and began to issue commands. His commands included Beverly and Christy. "You young ladies step back. We have animal control coming."

"Make sure they don't hurt him. Jon has had Walter forever, and we'd be in big trouble if anything happened to him," Beverly said.

Several of the other employees who were closing up their shops noticed all the commotion and came out to see what was happening. Within 10 minutes, the center of the mall was filled with people. Animal control arrived first, then the fire department with a paramedic backup unit, and a dozen curious onlookers.

After all that, Walter's capture turned out to be uneventful. An older man, dressed in padded gear, stepped into the planter, located Walter, and quickly extracted him with a long pole that had a sort of lasso on the end.

Wiggling his protest, the 15-foot runaway was marched back to his cage with a parade of followers. Beverly stayed behind to file a report with mall security, and Christy led the entourage to the pet store.

"Be careful," she warned, noticing the dog food still on the floor.

Walter was returned to his cage, the lock was secured, and for good measure, Christy placed a large bag of aquarium rocks over the top. Then she picked up the broom and went to work, sweeping up the dog food and trying to save as much as possible in a bucket.

Beverly returned, and the two young women laughed away the remainder of their tension.

"Should we tell Jon?" Beverly joked. "Or let him try to figure out why Walter suddenly has such a huge appetite?"

Christy laughed and glanced up at the clock. "Oh no! It's after 10:00! I have to call my parents."

Surely her parents would understand why she wasn't home by

10:00. They wouldn't put her on restriction for this, would they?

"Hello, Dad?"

"Where are you, Christy?"

"I'm still at work. You see, Walter was in the mall—"

"Walter?" Dad interrupted. "I thought you were going out with some guy named Rick."

Christy swallowed her laugh and said, "Dad, I can explain everything when I get home. I'm leaving right now."

She hung up and, laughing, told Beverly, "My dad thought Walter was my boyfriend!"

Beverly smiled back and said, "Maybe that's his way of telling you he thinks your boyfriend is a snake."

CHAPTER TEN

Wild Kites Dancing in the Wind

Not only were her parents understanding about her getting home so late, but they also entered into the adventure. Mom scooped up bowls of ice cream, and the three of them sat around the kitchen table while Christy described every detail of the great snake escape.

She hadn't noticed it at the time of her tumble, but Mom pointed out a big bruise already blackening above her right elbow. Christy also guessed her knee was bruised from the way it was throbbing.

"Too bad you're not going to work tomorrow," Mom said. "Your boss might have more sympathy if he saw your bruises."

"Why aren't you working tomorrow?" Dad asked.

"I'm going to the beach with Rick to fly kites, remember? You said it was okay."

"Oh, right," Dad said. "I forgot. Flying kites, huh? Where does this guy come up with all these creative ideas?"

Christy explained about Rick's list and how he wanted to ask her out for almost a year. It felt good telling Mom and Dad about this side of Rick. They couldn't help but think more highly of him for his persistence.

"Is this the same guy who called here on your birthday when you were in Hawaii and wanted your phone number?" Dad asked.

"Yes, that was Rick."

"Where was the kid calling from? Sounded as if he were at the end of a long tunnel."

"He was in Italy."

"You mean he called you in Maui, all the way from Italy?" Dad's bushy, red-brown eyebrows pushed up. "Maybe we've underestimated this guy."

The next morning Rick called at 11:10 to tell Christy he was running late. She had been ready since 10:30 and didn't feel like waiting around for him much longer.

"When do you think you'll be here?" she asked.

"As soon as I can. Some people dropped by. I can't leave yet, but I'll be over soon."

His "soon" turned out to be after 1:00. Christy had cleaned her room while waiting, her stomach gurgling its nervous anticipation the whole time. When she heard the doorbell ring, she felt like jerking open the door and ripping into Rick for being so late.

Mom let Rick in, and when Christy joined them, she masked her angry feelings and smiled at him as if nothing were wrong.

"The weather has certainly taken a turn today," Mom said. "Do you still think it's a good idea to go to the beach? It looks as though it might rain."

"This is the best time to fly kites," Rick answered, acting cool and confident. "I have a jacket in the car. Did you bring one, Christy?"

"No, I'll go get it."

How can he be so calm after making me wait for hours? I'd better relax or else I'm going to blow this whole day. He's here now, and that's all that matters.

She returned with a jacket and a smile, determined not to let anything ruin their time together. Her dad was now talking with Rick and her mom. Dad acted and sounded as if maybe he was warming up to Rick.

"Do you two want something to eat?" Mom asked.

"I thought we'd pick up some sandwiches for lunch, and then I told Christy I'd take her to Felicidades for dinner. They have the best Mexican food in Carlsbad. Have you ever been there?"

"No," Mom answered, "we'll have to try it sometime."

Christy had to admit she felt proud of the way Rick was nice to her parents after they had been so strict about her dating. In her opinion, they had also been downright rude to Rick.

"Have a great time, and we'll see you when you get home," Mom added.

"At 10:00," Rick added.

"Or even before 10:00," Christy's dad said. He was smiling.

It made Christy think of something Dad said last night after their ice cream. He told her that if being a teenager sometimes seemed difficult for her and she felt her parents were too strict, she should remember that they had never before been parents of a teen who could drive and date. Dad said he thought some things were scarier for him than they were for her. It wasn't as if he were experienced at all this and had the instant right answers.

As Rick and Christy got into the Mustang, David pedaled his bike to the side of the car. Before Rick could start the motor, David asked, "Where are you going? Can I go?"

Christy was used to David tagging along whenever she and Todd did things together, since she wasn't technically old enough to date then. Having David along tended to keep it from being a

date. Things were different now. She was on a date with her boyfriend and was about to say, "Sorry, David. Not this time," when
Rick answered for her.

"In your dreams, dog breath! Get your own life!" He revved
up the engine and screeched down the street.

Christy felt like scolding Rick and telling him he couldn't talk
to her brother like that. She also wanted to let him have it for
being so late. But she resisted the urge, not wanting to start off
their special day with an argument.

Rick opened the conversation. "I should have stayed with you
at the pet store last night instead of going to the football game.
Vista High beat us again."

"Did you go out afterward or anything?" Christy asked.

"Yeah. The usual place, the usual gang. Not much has
changed since last year. Oh, and Renee was all over me until I told
her we were going together. She'll probably look you up on Monday." He added in a mumble, "And by then you'll have proof."

Renee and Christy had had major conflicts last spring at
cheerleader tryouts, but this year their paths hadn't crossed much
yet. Christy had to admit, hearing that Rick had called her his
girlfriend in front of Renee felt satisfying.

"You like turkey?" Rick asked, parking in front of a sandwich
shop and opening Christy's door for her.

"I like you, don't I?" she teased, taking his hand and stepping
out of the car.

"Oh, cute. Very cute," Rick said, squeezing her hand and pulling it until her arm was around his middle. He wrapped his arm
around her waist and said, "So you think you're funny, huh?"
And he proceeded to tickle her mercilessly.

The laughing spell made her glad to be with Rick. They had
the rest of the day together, and she wanted to cherish every

minute of it. She could forgive him for being so late. After all, he did call and tell her he was running late.

They ate their sandwiches in the car on the way to the beach. As they drove, the sky became more overcast. It definitely did not look like a good day to go to the beach.

Rick parked in a dirt clearing near a precarious cliff that dropped off to the sand below. They put on their jackets and carried their kites down a path to the practically deserted beach.

"This is pretty," Christy said, surveying the long, narrow stretch of sand. "It's so different from Newport Beach. I've never been here before."

"You think we have enough wind for the kites?" Rick asked, fastening the string to the back of his.

The air felt thick and padded. A sliver of sun broke through the heavy clouds and struck the ocean like an iridescent javelin.

Rick handed Christy her kite. "Follow me. We're going to have to give these guys a running start."

Rick held his kite over his head and took off running down the beach. On the second try, his kite was airborne.

Christy followed Rick, and after six attempts, her kite took off. She let the string reel itself all the way out until the kite was only a colorful little triangle against the gray cotton-ball ceiling.

"That's us," Rick said, looking up. "Two wild kites dancing in the wind."

For a long time they stood, side by side, tugging on their strings and watching their kites whip and twist in the air. A few times their strings almost tangled together as the kites lunged toward each other and then pulled away.

"I don't think I've ever flown a kite before," Christy said, trying to link the present with some kind of memory from the past.

"I probably did when I was little, but I don't remember. This is really fun."

"So, you think number four was a good choice for today?" Rick said with a grin, referring to his date list.

"A very good choice. Although my arms are starting to feel tired."

"Here," Rick offered, taking her string. "Find us a couple of good rocks, and we'll anchor these guys down."

Christy had plenty of rocks to choose from. She lugged the closest two over to Rick's feet, where he secured the kite strings in the sand.

"That ought to hold them. You want to go for a walk?" Rick offered Christy his hand, and they started down the endless beach.

Feeling secure with her hand in Rick's, Christy opened up more than she had all day and began to tell him about the adventure with Walter the night before.

"Boy, am I sorry I missed all the excitement!" Rick said. "Wish I would have stuck around."

"Me, too."

Rick squeezed her hand. "It's been hard seeing you only once a week. I wish we could be together more. You don't have any idea what it means to me to be with you, Christy. I've waited so long to spend moments like this with you."

Rick stopped walking and looked at Christy with his warm brown eyes. "Sometimes I can't believe you're finally mine."

Then he wrapped his arms around her and kissed her.

Christy pulled away slightly, before he had a chance to kiss her again, hoping to catch her breath. As always, Rick came on too fast and too strong for her.

"Oh no, look!" she cried, pointing over his shoulder. "Our

kites are taking a dive into the water.''

Down the beach, the wind had changed, and both kites were losing altitude rapidly. They took crazy, gyrating swoops toward the incoming surf.

''They're okay,'' Rick said, pulling Christy toward him.

''Come on,'' Christy urged, ''we have to save them.'' She pulled away and started to run down the beach with Rick soon right beside her.

He's mad. I know it. He's mad that I pulled away. I'm still not used to him coming on to me like that. Does he really care about me, or is Katie and everyone else right? Is he going to use me until he's bored and then toss me away?

They reached the kites about the same time, but it was too late. The strings had become entangled, with both kites losing their momentum in the wind. Together they fell to earth at the edge of the shoreline, where the foamy waves rushed up to lick their paper wounds.

Christy examined the ruined bundle and wondered if they could be untangled and repaired. It didn't look too promising. They had crashed pretty hard.

''Well,'' Rick said lightheartedly, ''so much for wild kites dancing in the wind.'' He gathered them up and wadded them into a crumpled ball.

An unexpected tear slid down Christy's cheek as she watched Rick toss the fragile kites into the metal trash can.

CHAPTER ELEVEN

Tostada Surprise

After gathering their belongings and hiking back up the rocky hill, Christy enjoyed the warmth of Rick's car.

He didn't say much as they drove up the coast to Carlsbad. She wanted him to hold her hand and put on some soothing music, but he seemed deep in thought.

The moisture from the ocean mist had turned Rick's dark hair wavy and thick, making him look all the more rugged, like a mountain climber. She liked his hair this way and wondered if she should say something.

"We need to talk before we go to dinner," Rick said. "I want you to tell me everything you're feeling. There's too much that's going unsaid between us, and I want to clear everything up, okay?"

Christy nodded as he glanced at her. They parked in a paved area on a cliff overlooking the ocean. Rick turned off the engine of his Mustang and leaned against the window so he could face Christy.

She couldn't tell from his expression if he was angry or just serious.

"We've known each other about a year," Rick began. "From

113

the first time I met you, I knew you weren't like a lot of other girls. I don't know how you did it, but you got inside my head, and I thought about you all the time. Somebody told me you already had a boyfriend, but then I took a chance and asked you to homecoming, remember?"

Christy smiled. "Yes. I was so embarrassed to have to tell you I couldn't date until I was 16—a whole nine months away."

"And do you remember what I told you that day?" Rick's voice matched his soft expression.

Christy felt her heart turn into a marshmallow as she looked into Rick's eyes and said, "You told me that for a girl like me, you could wait that long."

"I meant it, Christy." Rick reached over and took her hand. "I've waited a long time to have you as my girlfriend. And now every time I try to hold you or kiss you, you pull away. Do you realize that ever since that night when you papered my house and jumped out of the bushes—man, you sure scared me—you've been running away from me? Why? I'm not going to hurt you. I promise. I only want to be close to you."

He looked as if his heart had turned to marshmallow, too. She had never realized Rick cared this deeply about her.

"I need to know why you won't let me hold you and kiss you. What's wrong with a guy showing his girlfriend how much he cares?"

How could Christy answer that? He made it sound so natural and innocent. How could she explain to him that she wanted to feel close to him, too, but that his kissing overpowered her? How could he understand her promise to Alissa to do nothing more than light kissing with a guy?

"I want you to open up to me, Christy. Tell me what you're thinking," Rick pleaded, squeezing her hand.

Christy decided to try a question. "This may sound really stupid, Rick, but what is your standard? Do you know what I mean? How far would you go with a girl?"

Rick looked surprised. "What are you getting at, Christy? You think I'm trying to take advantage of you?"

"No, not really." Christy felt embarrassed trying to talk about this with Rick. "I guess I kind of have a standard of not doing anything more than light kissing. And today on the beach, the way I started to feel when you were kissing me was, well, it felt like more than light kissing."

Rick's smile spread across his face. "So, I made you feel sick to your stomach again?"

Christy remembered how she had said that the night they parked at a place overlooking Escondido to admire the lights of city. It seemed to make Rick proud that he had such power over her.

"No, it's not that you make me sick to my stomach. I don't know how to explain it." Christy gathered courage to speak her mind. "You see, I love holding hands with you, and when you hug me, I feel warm and protected. Those things feel safe. The reason I keep pulling away, I guess, is because I don't want to go beyond that and get into a situation I can't get out of." The tangled kites came to her mind, but she decided to let her statement stand without adding the example.

"Okay," Rick said. He readjusted his position and acted as if their heart-to-heart discussion had come to an end. "Then that's what we'll do. Hold hands, hug, and kiss lightly."

The way he said it, it sounded as if he were making fun of her.

Starting the car, he added with a grin, "For now, that is."

Christy didn't know if her openness had given her a victory or had merely postponed a defeat. At any rate, she felt better, more settled and at ease with Rick, now that he knew where she drew the line and how she felt about things.

The Mexican restaurant was just beginning to seat guests for dinner. The hostess took them to a plush booth with high wooden backs covered in antique brocade fabric.

A man wearing an embroidered white shirt and a wide orange sash around the waist of his black pants brought them a basket of tortilla chips and filled their water glasses. "*Buenas noches,*" he said.

"Yeah, lots of nachos to you, too," Rick said. He scanned the menu. "You have to have the tostada."

"Oh, I do, do I? And who says I have to have a tostada?" Christy asked, her voice light and sassy.

"I do," Rick retorted, equally sassy. "Trust me. You want the tostada."

He slid to the edge of the booth and said, "I'll be right back. If the waiter comes, order me an iced tea and a number four combination."

Rick disappeared. The waiter appeared. Christy obediently ordered an iced tea and a number four for Rick. She hesitated, then gave in to Rick's directive and ordered a tostada and iced tea for herself.

Does this guy have power over me, or what?

Rick returned, all smiles. "You ordered the tostada, didn't you?"

"Yes, Your Majesty," Christy teased.

"What?" Rick looked startled that she would make such a comment. "You think I'm too demanding, or something?"

Christy smiled and said, "Or something."

He shrugged his shoulders and reached across the table to

hold her hand. "Must be that magnetic force I seem to have over you."

He barely touched his fingers to her hand and made an electrical buzzing sound. "Bzzzzt! Bzzzzt! Oh no, we're making a magnetic connection!" Meshing his fingers through hers, he said, "I can't seem to break loose! Oh no!" He twisted and jerked their linked hands back and forth as if an electrical current had permanently bonded them.

"Stop it," Christy said, smiling at his antics but inwardly feeling crushed that she had opened up her heart to him in the car, and now he was making fun of her for explaining why she had pulled away from him.

Rick relaxed their hands and said, "Do you know you have the softest hands of any girl I've ever known?"

Rick used his free hand to dip a tortilla chip into the ceramic saucer of salsa and said, "So, what do you want to do tomorrow? You have any great ideas, or should we keep working our way down my list?"

"Would you like to come over for dinner after church?" Christy asked, reaching for a chip.

"I'm not going to church. Didn't I already tell you? My brother and I have a racquetball match at 10:00. I could be to your house by 1:30, though."

It had been so long since Rick had been in church that Christy couldn't even remember the last time she had seen him there. It had to be some time back in June, before he went to Europe. Each week it was a different excuse. She didn't want to sound as if she were scolding him for not going to church anymore, so she said nothing and made a mental note to make sure he went with her next week.

The waiter approached their table with a steaming platter,

which he placed in front of Rick. Then, with a particularly toothy grin, the waiter said, *"Y señorita*, your tostada."

He set before her a plate heaped with a mountain of shredded lettuce, capped with a "snow peak" of sour cream. Something thick and silvery circled the lettuce just below the sour cream, catching the light and glimmering at her.

"What's this?" she asked, looking first at the waiter and then at Rick.

They both grinned like schoolboys with frogs in their pockets.

"Surprise!" Rick said, removing the silver ID bracelet from the lettuce mountain. "Let me put it on you."

He wiped off the sour cream with his napkin and placed the bracelet on Christy's right wrist, fastening the lock to make certain it was secure.

The waiter left them alone, and Rick, still grinning, said, "Do you like it?"

Christy looked at the wide silver bracelet now circling the wrist where for so many months she had worn Todd's bracelet. This one was thick and heavy. She held it toward the light and read the inscription in fancy scroll. It said, "RICK."

"Now there's no doubt who your boyfriend is," Rick said proudly. "You like it, don't you?"

"I'm just surprised, that's all. It's really nice. Thank you."

"I knew you'd like it better than the other one. A more-than-fair trade, I'd say," Rick said, picking up his fork and attacking the huge platter of food before him.

That comment hit Christy hard. It didn't just make her angry; it made her furious. Why was Rick so competitive and jealous that he had to replace Todd's bracelet with a bigger and better one, with his own name in bold letters on it?

She moved her tostada mountain around on her plate but

didn't eat much of it. Rick barely spoke at all but scarfed down his dinner, using the tortilla chips to scoop up the refried beans and rice.

Finally, Christy concluded within herself that replacing the ID bracelet was a guy kind of thing. It apparently made Rick feel more macho, as if he had marked his territory, and as he said, everyone would know that he was her boyfriend. Besides, being labeled as Rick's girlfriend wasn't a bad thing at all.

They left the restaurant hand in hand, the bracelet wedged between his hand and hers. It took only 10 minutes to drive across the freeway to the Cinema Center, where Rick led her to the box office. Without asking her opinion, he bought two tickets for a movie that was starting in five minutes.

"Good timing, huh?" Rick asked as they stepped out of line and headed for the door to turn in their tickets.

Christy hung back, reading the sign over the ticket window.

"Come on," Rick called to her.

She hurried to catch up, but just before he handed the tickets to the guy at the door, she pulled Rick's arm, drawing him off to the side.

"Rick," she said quietly, "that movie is rated R."

"So? I'm 18," Rick said.

"I'm not."

"You're with me. It doesn't matter. Nobody's going to ask you how old you are. Come on, we're going to miss the show."

"Rick," she said, letting her irritation show, "I can't watch that movie. I have an agreement with my parents that I won't go to R-rated shows."

"You're kidding," he said, laughing as if she were making a joke.

Christy stood her ground. "I'm serious, Rick."

People were watching their standoff.

"That does it!" Rick said, throwing his hands up in the air. He turned on his heel and stalked toward the parking lot.

Humiliated, Christy followed him to the car, feeling like a puppy with its tail between its legs.

As soon as they reached his car, where there wasn't an audience, Rick started to yell at her. "Why didn't you tell me your little rule before we got here? Why did you have to wait until we were at the door and make me feel like dirt in front of all those people? You are so full of rules, Christy. You're driving me crazy! You can't date until you're 16, then you have unrealistic curfews and get put on restriction for nothing. It's a major effort for you to even find the time to go out with me, and when you do, you have all these rules as if I'm some kind of monster you have to keep caged up! And now you won't even go to a stupid movie because it violates your perfect standards."

Rick kicked a tire and turned his fierce eyes on Christy. "You're being a baby. That's what you're doing. I know you, Christy. I've watched you for more than a year, and I know you're not a wimp, but you're wimping out on me."

He folded his arms across his chest. "So you'd better decide if you're ready to grow up and experience a real dating relationship or else . . . "

Christy couldn't contain her fiery emotions any longer. "Or else what? You'll dump me and find some other girl who'll do whatever you want? Is that what you were going to say? Go ahead. Say it."

Rick backed down, breathing heavily through his nose. "That's not what I want, and you know it. I want to go out with you."

Christy's feelings were at an all-time-high intensity, and she unleashed them. "You want to go out with me? Are you sure? You want me to be your girlfriend? Because if you do, then *this* is me! I have standards and rules and restrictions and everything else you just complained about. *That* is me, and if you want to date me, then you get the whole package, rules and all! I'm not going to change for you or any other guy."

Her whole body was shaking, but she mimicked his tough-guy stance by folding her arms and returning the hard look he had been giving her.

Rick unfolded his arms and stuck his hands in his pockets. He looked down at the pavement and shuffled some pebbles while he appeared to calm down.

Christy calmed down, too. She had amazed herself with the words that had spewed out of her mouth, but she didn't regret one of them. For the first time ever with Rick, she felt as if he were no longer in control.

"I was right," Rick said, looking at her sheepishly. "You're not a wimp. I shouldn't have blown up like that. I'm sorry."

"I'm sorry, too," Christy said automatically. She wasn't sure why she said it, because she really wasn't sorry for anything she said. She *was* sorry they had gone through such a scene, though.

Rick opened up his arms, inviting Christy to receive his hug. She willingly stepped into his embrace.

As he held her tightly, he said, "I do want to date you, just the way you are. I don't want you ever to change. You are one of a kind, Killer, and that's the way I want you to stay. I can learn to make a few adjustments, and maybe you can make a few, too."

They held each other long enough to feel calmed and restored. Christy lifted her head and said, "Do you still want to see a movie? There's one playing that's rated G."

"What, that animated one? Are you kidding?"

"No, I'm serious. Come on, it'll be fun," Christy urged.

Rick slowly gave in and walked back to the ticket booth with his arm around her shoulders. "I can see me telling my brother tomorrow on the racquetball court that I took my girlfriend to see a cartoon." Leaning down to speak to the girl in the ticket booth, he said, "Could we trade these two *adult* tickets for two tickets to the *kiddie* show?"

With the exchanged tickets in his hand, Rick led Christy to the door once more. Then, as if to make sure the guy collecting the tickets knew who was in control, Rick said, "I mean it, Christy. If I fall asleep in this one, you owe me a refund."

CHAPTER TWELVE

A Fair Trade?

Rick delivered Christy to her front door at five minutes to 10:00 and stated for the fifth time that the movie was "sweet."

"I'll be over around 1:30 tomorrow," he said. "Or do you want me to call first?"

"Better call just to make sure it's okay for you to come for lunch. What do you want to do tomorrow?" she asked.

"I'll check the list," he said, grasping her by the shoulders and planting a hard, fast kiss on her lips. "You'd better get in there before the clock strikes 10:00 and you turn into a pumpkin for another two weeks."

"Good night, Rick," she called as he jogged to his car. "See you tomorrow."

"Did you have a nice time?" Mom asked when Christy stepped inside.

"Yeah," she answered, not anxious to go into the details of the complicated day or to start answering questions about what the silver bracelet around her wrist meant. "I still have sand in my hair from the beach. I'm going to hop in the shower."

As Christy washed her hair, Rick's bracelet became tangled in it. She ended up yanking out a chunk of hair. Todd's bracelet never did that.

Thinking of Todd's bracelet made her wonder where she had put it. The last time she had seen it was when Rick took it off at the restaurant and she had slipped it into her black clutch purse.

After her shower, she pulled the purse out of her drawer and dumped its contents onto her bed. Lipstick, mascara, tissue, a quarter, and a pen. No bracelet. She swished her hand around the inside of the fabric lining to see if it had caught there. Still no bracelet.

She went to the drawer where the purse had been and ran the palm of her hand inside the drawer in case it had fallen out of the purse. No bracelet.

She grabbed the Folgers coffee can off her dresser and emptied out the dried-up carnation petals from the first bouquet Todd had given her, remembering that she had buried the bracelet in there once before. It wasn't there.

What did I do with it? I put it in my purse, then I left my purse in Rick's car, and he gave it back to me the next night. Could it have fallen out in his car?

Christy worked the purse's clasp back and forth. It was strong and couldn't have opened on its own.

She was beginning to panic. Scooping the dried carnations back into the coffee tin, she hurriedly returned it to its spot on her dresser.

The coffee tin collided with the blue pottery vase, knocking it off her dresser. Hitting the edge of her desk, the vase shattered into a dozen pieces on the floor.

Oh no! Not Rick's vase! How am I going to tell him I broke it?

She gathered up the shards of jagged pottery, wondering if she could glue them back together. The roses had died a week ago, and Christy had tossed them out, not even thinking of saving them the way she had Todd's carnations.

Todd, Rick, flowers, broken vases, lost bracelets—all like the pieces of broken pottery she tried to match up on the floor.

Christy gave up trying to piece the broken vase together and put it all in the trash can. She crawled under her covers and held her stuffed Winnie the Pooh bear that Todd had given her on her fifteenth birthday.

That was the night she had prepared herself for her very first kiss when Todd walked her to the door, only he didn't kiss her. He did kiss her the day he gave her the bouquet of carnations. She was leaving for the airport to go back to Wisconsin, and Todd had kissed her in the middle of the street in front of a whole bunch of people. His kiss had made her feel fresh and free, not like he was trying to "magnetize" her.

For more than an hour she lay with Pooh in her arms, thinking through all the comparisons and differences between Rick and Todd. For so long she had wanted Todd to be the kind of boyfriend Rick was being to her now. Yet Todd would never hold her or pressure her or say things to her the way Rick did.

Now she had what she had wanted for so long—a boyfriend, Rick. Rick adored her so much he even sat through a "kiddie" movie with her. He held her and kissed her and said things that made her feel beautiful. Rick had made a list of possible dates, he had brought her roses, and he had given her a bracelet.

Rick wanted her in his life. Todd had left her. Sure, things were bumpy with Rick, but they kept working at their relationship, and that's what really mattered. Things were getting better. Weren't they?

Even though her relationship with Todd was over, it still bothered her that she couldn't find his bracelet. She couldn't explain why, but that bracelet meant more to her than Rick's did. She had to find it.

Maybe it had fallen on the floor in Rick's car. Maybe Rick had it and just hadn't told her. She decided she would ask him tomorrow.

Christy's parents agreed that Rick could come for lunch, and Mom kept the meal warm in the oven, waiting for him to call.

He finally phoned at 2:00, saying his racquetball game had run late. He suggested they go ahead and eat, since he still had to shower and wouldn't be there for another 45 minutes or so.

The family ate the dried-out chicken and cool mashed potatoes without much conversation. Dad retired to read the Sunday paper and take his customary snooze on the couch. Christy did the dishes and then went out front to wait for Rick. She didn't want him bounding up the steps and waking her dad.

She had Rick's bracelet in the pocket of her cutoff jeans. She hadn't worn it all day because she wasn't ready to answer the questions it would have raised at church or with her parents.

Christy waited patiently on the top step of the porch. Fall was definitely coming. The night-blooming jasmine that covered the trellis above her head had withered, and the vine was filled with hundreds of tiny brown squiggles where fragrant white flowers had once bloomed.

She could hear Rick's Mustang before she saw it turn the corner of her quiet street. She hurried down to the street to meet it.

"Hi," she said brightly through the open passenger window. "Who won?"

"Do you need to ask? I did, of course. My brother's ticked, too. He's three years older than I am, and he hasn't been able to beat me at anything for the last six months."

"I can believe that," Christy said. "My dad's asleep, and I

think my mom is sewing. Do you want me to see if we can go somewhere?"

"Sure. We'll go over to my house. Hey, where's my bracelet?"

"In my pocket. I'll be right back." She ran in the house, grabbed a sweatshirt, and asked Mom if she could go to Rick's.

"As long as you're back before 6:00," Mom said. "And do you have any homework you need to finish this weekend?"

She had forgotten all about her mound of homework. "Some," she answered cautiously. "I'll do it when I get back. Bye." She quickly scooted out before Mom had time to say anything else.

Once in the car with Rick, she tied her sweatshirt around her waist and, pulling the bracelet from her pocket, explained how it had become tangled in her hair the night before. A hair strand was still twisted around the clasp.

"Here," Rick said. "I'll put it back on you. You'll have to be more careful when you wash your hair."

Rick locked the clasp and then started the car. They had driven about three blocks toward the expensive side of town, where Rick lived, when Christy decided to ask Rick if he had come across Todd's bracelet.

"Rick, I wanted to ask you something," Christy said cautiously. The last thing she needed was for him to get mad because she was talking about Todd.

"Good," Rick said, pulling the car into a parking lot behind a complex of doctors' offices, "because I wanted to ask you something, too."

He turned off the car and reached his arms around her, then kissed her slowly and gently. Pulling back, he asked, "How was that for 'light kissing'? I'm getting better, aren't I?"

"Rick," Christy said, thinking she had better talk fast before her emotions clouded, "remember the night we went to that Italian restaurant?"

"You looked gorgeous," he said. "I loved you in that black dress."

"Rick, come on! Let me ask this and get it over with. That night you took off my gold ID bracelet, and I put it in my purse. I left my purse in your car, then you gave it back to me the next night when you drove me home."

Rick leaned against his door. "Yeah, so what?" He sounded defensive.

"I wondered if you saw the bracelet after that. I thought it might have fallen out of my purse onto the floor or something. Have you seen it?"

"You don't need it anymore."

"But I don't like not knowing where it is. I'd feel awful if I lost it."

"Why?" Rick challenged. "Why do you even want to know where it is?"

"Because it's a valuable bracelet, and I don't like to go around misplacing valuable things."

"Calm down," Rick said, putting his arms back around her. "You don't need to get all upset about such a little thing." He spoke softly in her ear. "You're my girlfriend now. You don't need to worry about that jerk anymore. You have me."

Christy's anger flared. Todd was a lot of things, but he was not a jerk. True, she had called Todd names before in her mind, and "jerk" had been one of them. But that was different. She could call Todd a jerk, but Rick couldn't.

"Pretty good trade, don't you think? Me for 'Moondoggie.' My bracelet for his."

Rick's last phrase played again in her mind like sour organ

notes in a monster movie. *My bracelet for his.*

Grabbing his wide shoulders and looking him in the eye, she demanded, "Tell me the truth, Rick Doyle. Did you take my bracelet out of my purse?"

Rick put on an easygoing grin and said calmly, "Come on, Christy, relax. You didn't need that thing anymore. You have my bracelet now."

"You did!" she screamed in his face. "You took my bracelet! You had no right to do that. You can't just go into a girl's purse and take what isn't yours and keep it. How dare you! Where is it? I want it back right now!"

Rick looked shocked at her outburst, then he opened fire on her. "You know what your problem is? You aren't mature enough to handle a real dating relationship! You want to keep all your childhood trinkets and let a perfect relationship go out the window."

"Where's my bracelet, Rick?" Her voice had changed to a low growl.

He stuck out his jaw and looked away from her.

"Where's my bracelet, Rick?"

"You're really making me angry, Christy."

She spoke her words with staccato force. "Where-is-my-bracelet?"

"I don't have it, all right?" he yelled, drawing himself up straight in his seat and pointing his finger at her. "You decide right here, right now. Who's it going to be? Me or that surfer jerk? You decide right now, and that's it! Who's it going to be? Tell me!"

Christy had never seen him this angry, and it terrified her. She acted on impulse, opening her car door and taking off running.

"Fine!" he hollered. "Go ahead and run. Only this time,

Christy Miller, I'm not running after you!"

Hearing his car start, she ran between the buildings so he couldn't follow her down the sidewalk. She stopped at a bench in the deserted office complex and caught her breath. Once it sounded as though his car was gone, she started to walk home.

I can't believe this is happening! Did I do the right thing by jumping out of the car? He's so mad he probably won't speak to me for a week. What if he calls? What will I say? I can't help it! I'm still mad he took Todd's bracelet.

When she reached the front of the office complex, there was Rick leaning against his parked car.

"This is crazy," he said. "Why are we doing this? Come on, get in the car. Let's talk this through." Rick's voice was calm and persuasive.

Christy stood still, staring at her shoes. She didn't want to get in the car. She felt too shaken to let him smooth this one over.

Without looking up, she calmly restated her question. "Where's my bracelet, Rick?"

"You know," he said in a broken voice, "I thought I was doing the best thing for us. I really did." He sounded as though he was about to cry.

Christy battled with whether she should keep her distance or go to his side and comfort him. She stayed several feet away but spoke softly. "What did you do, Rick?"

"I didn't want anything to come between us. I had no idea that bracelet meant so much to you. I took it to the jewelry store and traded it for the one I gave you."

"You traded it?" Christy said in a whisper. Then, with firm, angry words, she said, "You had no right to do that."

"I know. I realize that now. At the time I thought it was the best thing for our relationship," Rick said briskly. "I'm sorry."

She couldn't tell if he was truly sorry or only sorry the trade had backfired on him.

"You don't have to compete with everybody in the world, Rick. You don't have to be jealous of Todd. He's thousands of miles away."

"No he's not," Rick said quickly. "He's still in your head. I can tell. He's competition. He always has been."

"I can't believe this! Rick, I'm dating you, not Todd. Can't you see how much I've wanted to be with you?"

"What is it about him? Why is he still so important to you? Did he write you love poems or make big promises about your future?"

Christy couldn't help but laugh. "No. Todd has never written me a letter or note of any kind. And he is about the most non-committal person I've ever known."

"Then what's the deal with him? What makes you so drawn to him?"

Christy had to think about it. Rick was right; some kind of bond existed between her and Todd. How could she explain it?

"I think it's the Lord," Christy said finally. "I think what makes Todd unique is that he prays with me and—"

Rick cut in. "We can pray. Is that what you want?"

Christy realized that during the entire time she had known Rick and had been dating him, they had never prayed or even talked about the Lord or spiritual things. "Yeah, I'd like it a lot if we prayed together. But it's not just that. It's . . ."

In trying to find the words to explain Todd's uniqueness, she remembered how Todd would look when he talked about God. It was a contented, vulnerable, strong-as-a-rock look. That was it. Todd loved Jesus more than anything. How could she explain that to Rick?

"Come here," Rick invited, holding out his right hand. "Do you want to try praying with me?"

Christy placed her hands in his. Rick bowed his head and closed his eyes. Then he prayed, "Our almighty heavenly Father, we come to You asking for strength and direction in our relationship. Please grant us Your blessing and help us to work through all our problems. Amen."

He lifted his head and looked at her like a little kid waiting for approval. It wasn't anything at all like the way Todd prayed. Nothing about Rick was like Todd. She suddenly realized nothing ever would be. Rick was Rick. Did she really want to be his girl-friend?

"Do you want to go over to my house now? We can pretend all this never happened and start over," Rick said.

"Actually . . ." Christy forced herself to finish her sentence be-fore she chickened out. "I think we should break up."

Rick looked at her as if she had told a bad joke. "But we just prayed. And I told you I was sorry about the bracelet. Why would you want to break up?"

"Because I don't think I'm ready to be your girlfriend. I don't think I'm ready to be anybody's girlfriend. I want to go back to being your friend. We got along so much better when we were friends."

Rick ran his fingers through his hair and looked frantic. "I don't get it. I'm trying to do everything right. I've never, ever tried this hard with any girl before. What am I doing wrong?"

"It's not you. It's me. You've said it a couple of times: I'm not ready to have a serious dating relationship. I'd like to slow down everything. It seems as though you went from being my buddy to my boyfriend overnight, and that's too fast for me. I think it would be better if we built up our relationship slowly."

"We have been building it up slowly," Rick said. "Or did you forget the nine months I waited to date you?"

"That's exactly it, though. I thought you were waiting to *date* me, not possess me. I'm not ready to go steady—with anybody. I need time for myself, and I want to spend time with my girl-friends without feeling that I have to ask your permission."

Christy thought of other things she wanted to say, but Rick looked so wounded she decided to stop there. He obviously got the point. It surprised her how calm and peaceful she felt for someone who had just broken up with her boyfriend, especially since none of this had been planned or decided ahead of time.

"You know," Rick said, drawing himself up to his full height and looking down on Christy, "I have a lot of pressures on me, with starting college and all. I think we should slow things down and give each other a chance to catch up with everything in our lives. I don't know when I'll be back up here for the weekend. Thanksgiving, probably not before. I'll give you a call then. Maybe we can get together and go somewhere just to talk. The time will give us a chance to reevaluate our relationship."

Christy thought it was kind of funny to watch Rick take con-trol of the situation, speaking smooth words like the closing lines of a movie. The way he restated everything, it sounded as though he were the one breaking up with her.

"I'll look forward to your call," she said.

Rick looked at her as though she were patronizing him.

"No, really, I will! We still have a whole list of dates that you thought up, remember? And I'd like to go on them with you. We can take them one at a time instead of trying to do them all in one week."

Christy tried to sound as light and positive as she could, be-cause her emotions were catching up with her prior burst of logic, and she felt a major storm brewing inside.

"I think you should have the bracelet back. I'm always going to be your friend, Rick. But I can't be your girlfriend right now. Could you help me take it off?"

Rick picked the clasp with his thumb and held the bracelet in his fist. "I'm holding on to this," he said tenderly, "because I still think it belongs on your wrist. One day I want to put it back there."

His last statement felt like a clap of thunder, releasing the storm inside Christy. She lowered her head as tears fell on the pavement.

"Can I give my friend a hug?" Rick asked.

Christy nodded without looking up.

He wrapped his big arms around her and hugged her good-bye.

CHAPTER THIRTEEN

Twice

Monday morning Christy wanted to stay in bed and skip school. She hadn't touched her homework all weekend, and she was emotionally exhausted. How could she convince Mom that she was sick and needed to stay home?

Her mother saw right through Christy's scheme and gave her 20 minutes to get dressed and out the door.

Christy threw on a sweater and jeans and pulled back her hair in a braid. This was definitely not going to be one of her more glamorous days.

She slid through the first two classes, begging extended time on one of her homework assignments. Third period, she wasn't so fortunate.

"Today, class," her literature teacher began, "we shall start our readings of the Victorian poems you've selected. Our first reader will be Christy Miller."

"I left my book in my locker," Christy answered, hoping she could get off the hook.

"That's half a grade off. Take a hall pass to get your book, and let's see if you can manage a passing grade. While Christy gets her book, does anyone else have to retrieve a book from his or her locker?''

When Christy returned to class, another girl was reading her selection, tripping over the *thee*s and *thou*s.

Christy had barely found the right page when the teacher called on her to stand and read. She wished she would have at least looked the poem over before having to read it in front of the class—especially on a day when she looked and felt so yucky.

'' 'Twice,' by Christina Rossetti,'' Christy began and then read,

> I took my heart in my hand
> (O my love, O my love),
> I said: Let me fall or stand,
> Let me live or die,
> But this once hear me speak—
> (O my love, O my love)—
> Yet a woman's words are weak;
> You should speak, not I.
> You took my heart in your hand
> With a friendly smile,
> With a critical eye you scanned,
> Then set it down,
> And said: It is still unripe,
> Better wait awhile;
> Wait while the skylarks pipe,
> Till the corn grows brown.
> As you set it down it broke—
> Broke, but I did not wince;
> I smiled at the speech you spoke,
> At your judgment that I heard:
> But I have not often smiled

Since then, nor questioned since,
Nor cared for corn-flowers wild,
Nor sung with the singing bird.
I take my heart in my hand,
O my God, O my God,
My broken heart in my hand:
Thou hast seen, judge Thou.
My hope was written on sand,
O my God, O my God;
Now let Thy judgment stand—
Yea, judge me now.
This contemned of a man,
This marred one heedless day,
This heart take Thou to scan
Both within and without:
Refine with fire its gold,
Purge Thou its dross away—
Yea hold it in Thy hold,
Whence none can pluck it out.
I take my heart in my hand—
I shall not die, but live—
Before Thy face I stand;
I, for Thou callest such:
All that I have I bring,
All that I am I give,
Smile Thou and I shall sing,
But shall not question much.

At about the fourth line of her reading, Christy had realized
how similar this poem was to all that she had been through with
Todd and Rick during the last month. She had chosen the poem
from the list because it was written by a Christina. But now she

knew it wasn't an accident. Katie would call this a "God-thing."

With a heartfelt interest in the poem, Christy read with tearful intensity, as though she had practiced the reading all weekend. And in a way, maybe she had.

When she finished, her teacher stood up and, clasping her hands together, said, "Now *that* is an exceptional reading! Thank you, Christy, thank you!"

When the bell rang and the students herded through the hall, Katie caught up to Christy and said, "When did you have time to practice your reading? I thought you were with Rick all weekend."

"I didn't practice. I lived it." As generally as possible, Christy gave Katie a quick rundown on the weekend.

"So you can be happy that I'm no longer going out with Rick, since you never did like us being together," Christy concluded.

"That wasn't it," Katie protested. "I didn't want him breaking your heart, that's all. I'm glad you broke up with him instead of the other way around. I will admit that. I just didn't want to see you hurt."

"Then close your eyes," Christy said, "because I'm hurt."

After school she called her mom and asked if she could go to the mall to pick up her paycheck, since she hadn't worked Saturday. Even though Christy did want her paycheck, she had another reason for going. She entered the mall and headed straight for the jewelry store.

"May I help you?" asked an older, balding man behind the counter.

"I hope so," Christy said. "A week or so ago, a guy named Rick Doyle apparently came in here and traded in a small, gold ID bracelet. He bought a silver one instead. I was wondering if, by any chance, you still have the gold bracelet."

"Let me check," the man said and disappeared into the back of the shop.

When he returned, he had a long, thin box in his hand. Opening up the velvet-lined case, he held the bracelet for her to see and said, "Is this it?"

Christy's heart jumped, as if she'd spotted an old friend in a crowd. "Yes, that's it. I can't believe you still have it! May I have it back? I mean, I'd like to buy it back."

"I'm sure we can arrange that," the man said, checking the tag now attached to the chain. "That will be $145.50, plus tax."

"A hundred and forty-five dollars? That can't be right!"

"This is a valuable bracelet, miss."

"You're telling me," she mumbled.

"Apparently, it was handmade. We've checked all our manufacturers' catalogs, and this is not a standard issue. That doubles the price. Plus it's 24-karat gold, not the usual 14-karat. It's one of a kind."

Christy tried to respond as graciously as possible. "I know it is, sir. You see, that is my bracelet. The guy I mentioned earlier stole it out of my purse and brought it to you without my knowing about it. He gave me a silver one to replace it, but it's just not the same."

"I see," the man said. "And have you reported this theft to the proper authorities? We do have a procedure we can follow for this sort of thing if you haven't already pressed charges."

Christy had to admit that for one minute it was tempting to press charges against Rick. "No, I haven't reported it, and I don't think I want to. I'd simply like my bracelet back."

"Did you bring in the silver one to exchange?"

"No, I don't have that one."

"How would you like to pay for this, then? Cash, check, or

charge?" The man looked as if he knew she had none of them to offer.

"I'd like to pay cash, but I don't have enough yet," Christy explained.

"I see," the man said, snapping the case shut on the bracelet.

"I work across the mall at the pet store, and I get paid every Saturday. Could I put some money down on the bracelet today, and then every week pay what I can until it's all paid for?" Christy tried to look as sincere as possible so the man would see she meant business.

"We could do a layaway for you. We would need 10 percent today, and you could continue to make payments until it's paid off."

"Okay," Christy agreed, mentally calculating what 10 percent would be. "I'll go cash my check and be right back."

"Fine. I'll hold the bracelet for you."

The rest of the week dragged by slowly, silently. The phone didn't ring, her parents asked few questions, and Christy spent each afternoon and evening buried in homework.

Her heart and mind continually battled over Rick.

Why did I ever break up with him? We could have worked it out. Every couple has problems. Why did I push him away? Am I just running from him again, or did I really do the right thing?

Of course I did the right thing! Our relationship was headed down the wrong road, and the farther I would have walked down that road with Rick, the longer and harder it would have been to get back.

But back to what? Todd?

This is all a cruel joke. Here I am, finally old enough to date, and the only two guys I've ever cared about I've pushed right out of my life.

The biggest blow came on Wednesday when Renee, the cheer-leader Rick had mentioned during the weekend, came marching up to Christy at lunch. She had two of her friends with her.

Tapping Christy on the shoulder, she said, "So, let's see your proof."

"What are you talking about?" Christy asked.

"Yeah," Katie jumped in to defend Christy.

"I want to see your proof. Rick said you two were going together, and I told him I'd believe it when I saw it. He told me to find you this week, and you'd have evidence."

Katie interrupted, apparently trying to protect Christy. "It's not any of your business who Christy is going with."

"You're not going with him, are you?" Renee taunted. "Rick has been after you for so long he's having hallucinations that he's going with you. Why don't you tell Rick to wake up and start dating someone who's more his style—like me."

"Rick is free to date whomever he wants," Christy said quietly.

"So you're not going with him, are you?" Renee turned to the girls with her. "See? I told you guys. I knew it all along."

"Well, for your information—" Katie began.

"Katie." Christy tried to stop her, but it was no use.

"Christy and Rick *were* going together. The evidence was a very expensive bracelet he gave her on one of their many dates out to dinner at expensive restaurants." Katie picked up steam. "But Christy gave it back to him and broke up with him because she saw right through that egotistical jerk!"

Oh, Katie, I wish you would've kept your mouth shut.

Renee looked at Christy in disbelief. "You mean you had him? You had Rick Doyle in the palm of your hand, and you let him go?"

"It was a mutual decision," Christy said softly.

A smug looked crossed Renee's face as she said, "You don't

have to explain it to me. You'll get over him. And hey, if you're going to wait until you're 16 to lose your virginity, it might as well be with a guy like Rick . . . even if he did dump you once he got what he wanted."

Christy and Katie both shot up from the picnic table like twin rockets and faced Renee.

"I did *not* lose my virginity," Christy said, her words flaming hot.

"Not that it's any of your business," Katie said.

Renee laughed at them. "You mean you didn't do it with Rick? I can't believe you're such a loser! What is your problem, Christy?"

"You're the one with the problem, Renee," Katie popped off.

Then Christy said firmly, "The way I see it, Renee, you're the loser. You see, I can become like you anytime, not that I want to. But you can never become a virgin like me again."

Christy thought Renee was going to slap her. Renee spun around and marched off.

Katie and Christy sat back down and exchanged looks that said, "Can you believe what just happened?" Christy felt yucky inside. She was normally a private person, yet during the past few days she'd yelled at Rick in a parking lot and now she'd blasted Renee in public. This was not the way Christy wanted to handle her relationships.

Katie kept muttering about Renee and how she acted as though the world revolved around her. Christy closed her eyes and wished all this confronting and criticizing would just go away.

It took several days before all the uncomfortable feelings started to go away. By the week's end, it turned out to be a good thing Christy had to work Friday and Saturday. The routine of the pet store helped keep her preoccupied and made her feel more emotionally stable.

The store was busy all day Saturday. Christy sold 25 tropical fish to one man, who said he had a six-foot aquarium at home. On her break, Christy cashed her check and went to the jewelry store to make another payment on her bracelet. The check had been very small, since she hadn't worked the previous Saturday.

"I only have $21 to put toward my bracelet this week," Christy explained to the salesman. "I'll have the usual amount next week. I hope it's okay."

"Yes, it's fine. I checked with Jon, and he told me you're a dependable employee."

Christy smiled her thanks. "So, after this payment, how much more do I owe?"

The man scribbled on a piece of paper and said, "At this rate, you could have it paid for by Thanksgiving."

"Good," Christy said, remembering that Rick had said he would be home at Thanksgiving. Maybe, just maybe, Todd would be home for the holiday, too. "I'd like to have it back on my wrist by then."

When work ended, Christy had to swing past the library to return her poetry book. The night before she had copied the poem "Twice" into her diary and thought again of how she had felt that morning on the beach when she had offered her heart to Todd and he had set it down, telling her it was not yet "ripe."

I wonder what she was like, the Christina who wrote that poem? I wonder who the guy was who broke her heart? It's weird to think she lived more than a hundred years ago, yet the same things she felt are what I'm feeling now.

Christy was a few blocks from the library when she noticed she was driving right by the park Rick had taken her to. It was after 6:00, and the playground was empty. On impulse, she pulled into the parking lot, parked the car, and made her way through the sand to the empty swings.

At first she sat in a swing, just rocking back and forth slowly, etching circles in the sand with her tennis shoes.

A gentle autumn breeze rustled the trees, sending a flurry of dancing leaves into the air. Several of them fluttered down to Christy's feet. The once-green leaves had changed to a smear of oranges, yellows, and reds.

"We're changing, that's all. We're both changing." Todd's words from that morning on the beach came back to her as she picked up one of the leaves and examined it more closely.

The tree isn't dead; it's just changing. There will be new growth in the spring. Maybe that's how it'll be for Todd and me.

Christy let the leaf go. A puff of wind caught it and carried it spinning through the air until it landed on the grass.

"Father," she prayed in a whisper, "You know how much thinking I've been doing this past week. I keep coming to the same conclusion. I need to fall in love with You. I need to be content with just You as my first love. I'm not ready for a steady relationship with any guy until I'm first secure in my love for You.

"I want to love You with all my heart, soul, strength, and mind. I want to be more in love with You than I've ever been in love with anyone or anything. What did that poem say? 'All that I have I bring. All that I am I give. Smile Thou, and I shall sing but shall not question much.' "

As she prayed, Christy was slowly pumping her legs out and back. Without realizing it, she had gained altitude and was swinging pretty high. When the swing went forward, she hit a spot where the evening sun sliced through the trees and shot a beam of golden light on her face.

Up and back, up and back. Each time she swung forward, the sun shone on her face.

"The Lord make His face to shine upon you . . ." Those were Todd's words—his blessing.

In an amazing way, it was coming true. Christy felt as if the Lord's face were shining on her. And now that she thought about it, God had given her His peace.

What was that last part of Todd's blessing? Something about loving the Lord above all else.

For the first time all week, a smile found its way to Christy's lips. She pushed herself higher and higher in the swing until she felt the exhilarating rush of the wind through her hair. Then pointing her toes out straight and leaning back in the soaring swing, Christy sang out a spontaneous love song to the Lord of forever as her heart filled with hope.

Don't Miss These Captivating Stories in
The Christy Miller Series

#1 • Summer Promise
Christy spends the summer at the beach with her wealthy aunt and uncle. Will she do something she'll later regret?

#2 • A Whisper and a Wish
Christy is convinced that dreams do come true when her family moves to California and the cutest guy in school shows an interest in her.

#3 • Yours Forever
Fifteen-year-old Christy does everything in her power to win Todd's attention.

#4 • Surprise Endings
Christy tries out for cheerleader, learns a classmate is out to get her, and schedules two dates for the same night.

#5 • Island Dreamer
It's an incredible tropical adventure when Christy celebrates her 16th birthday on Maui.

#6 • A Heart Full of Hope
A dazzling dream date, a wonderful job, a great car. And lots of freedom! Christy has it all. Or does she?

#7 • True Friends
Christy sets out with the ski club and discovers the group is thinking of doing something more than hitting the slopes.

#8 • Starry Night
Christy is torn between going to the Rose Bowl Parade with her friends or on a surprise vacation with her family.

#9 • Seventeen Wishes
Christy is off to summer camp—as a counselor for a cabin of wild fifth-grade girls.

#10 • A Time to Cherish
A surprise houseboat trip! Her senior year! Lots of friends! Life couldn't be better for Christy until . . .

#11 • Sweet Dreams
Christy's dreams become reality when Todd finally opens his heart to her. But her relationship with her best friend goes downhill fast when Katie starts dating Michael, and Christy has doubts about their relationship.

#12 • A Promise Is Forever
On a European trip with her friends, Christy finds it difficult to keep her mind off Todd. Will God bring them back together?

THE SIERRA JENSEN SERIES

If you've enjoyed reading about Christy Miller,
you'll love reading about Christy's friend Sierra Jensen.

#1 • Only You, Sierra
When her family moves to another state, Sierra dreads going to a new high school—until she meets Paul.

#2 • In Your Dreams
Just when events in Sierra's live start to look up—she even gets asked out on a date—Sierra runs into Paul.

#3 • Don't You Wish
Sierra is excited about visiting Christy Miller in California during Easter break. Unfortunately, her sister, Tawni, decides to go with her.

#4 • Close Your Eyes
Sierra experiences a sticky situation when Paul comes over for dinner and Randy shows up at the same time.

#5 • Without A Doubt
When handsome Drake reveals his interest in Sierra, life gets complicated.

#6 • With This Ring
Sierra couldn't be happier when she goes to Southern California to join Christy Miller and their friends for Doug and Tracy's wedding.

#7 • Open Your Heart
When Sierra's friend Christy Miller receives a scholarship from a university in Switzerland, she invites Sierra to go with her and Aunt Marti to visit the school.

#8 • Time Will Tell
After an exciting summer in Southern California and Switzerland, Sierra returns home to several unsettled relationships.

#9 • Now Picture This
When Sierra and Paul start corresponding, she imagines him as her boyfriend and soon begins neglecting her family and friends.

#10 • Hold On Tight
Sierra joins her brother and several friends on a road trip to Southern California to visit potential colleges.

#11 • Closer Than Ever
When Paul doesn't show up for her graduation party and news comes that a flight from London has crashed, Sierra frantically worries about the future.

#12 • Take My Hand
A costly misunderstanding leaves Sierra anxious as she says goodbye to Portland and heads off to California for her freshman year of college.

FOCUS ON THE FAMILY®
ℒIKE THIS BOOK?

Then you'll love *Brio* magazine! Written especially for teen girls, it's packed each month with 32 pages on everything from fiction and faith to fashion, food . . . even guys! Best of all, it's all from a Christian perspective! But don't just take our word for it. Instead, see for yourself by requesting a complimentary copy.

Simply write Focus on the Family, Colorado Springs, CO 80995 (in Canada, write P.O. Box 9800, Stn. Terminal, Vancouver, B.C. V6B 4G3) and mention that you saw this offer in the back of this book. You may also call 1-800-232-6459 (in Canada, call 1-800-661-9800).

You may also visit our Web site (www.family.org) to learn more about the ministry or find out if there is a Focus on the Family office in your country.

Want to become everyone's favorite baby-sitter? Then *The Ultimate Baby-Sitter's Survival Guide* is for you! It's packed with page after page of practical information and ways to stay in control; organize mealtime, bath time and bedtime; and handle emergency situations. It also features an entire section of safe, creative and downright crazy indoor and outdoor activities that will keep kids challenged, entertained and away from the television. Easy-to-read and reference, it's the ideal book for providing the best care to children, earning money and having fun at the same time.

Call Focus on the Family at the number above, or check out your local Christian bookstore.

Focus on the Family is an organization that is dedicated to helping you and your family establish lasting, loving relationships with each other and the Lord. It's why we exist! If we can assist you or your family in any way, please feel free to contact us. We'd love to hear from you!